Hot Property

An Onalee O'Conner Mystery

By Connie Doherty

Connie Doherty

Copyright© 2016 - Connie Doherty

Publisher: The Dancing Turtle Press

Cover Artist: Meredith Krell

Published in the United States of America

ISBN 978-0-9975251-0-6

For Gloria Eli, Barb Hogarth, Linda Carapelluci, Ian Buckley, Kara Rosen, Cleon McLaughlin, Jeff and Tom Petz, Yu Teng, and everyone else who made playing badminton a magical experience for me.

Chapter One

You'd think after reading 841 detective novels that I, Onalee O'Conner, would know what to do when a dead body pops up. But, a dead body in person proves to be more trouble than I'd ever imagined.

*****

All morning long I had been hithering and yonning and whirling and dervishing. As a commercial real estate appraiser, I spent many of my days in the field, researching clues, tracking down elusive leads, calculating and working to crack the puzzle of a property's value. As my friend Marti and I often say, we appraisers do the grueling work of a private eye, but without all of the glitz and glamour.

I now live in Petoskey, a small resort town, south of the Mackinac Bridge in Michigan's Lower Peninsula. As the Yoopers, people from the Upper Peninsula, would say, I live under the bridge and that makes me a troll. Of course they're the same people who keep talking secession. From Michigan. They want to form their own state, not called something appropriate, like Cedar-Swamp-Arkania or No-Mans-Landia. Oh no, if they have their way, their mighty state, with about one Yooper family per one-hundred square miles, would be the grand state of Superior. It's as clear a case of Peninsula Envy as I've ever seen.

I had grown up in Petoskey and moved back here from Metropolitan Detroit, about three years ago. Lately, my hometown has occasionally been ranked on lists of The Top 100 Places to Live. What the lists don't tell is the old Petoskey saying, "A view of the bay is half the pay." This is why I, and a lot of my friends, left the area. But the town, my personal "City by the Bay", gets in your blood.

Getting back to me, they're now calling fifty the new thirty. Ergo, I'm a twenty-something single woman. I'm currently between dating opportunities, though I definitely have my eye on someone. I have my own house, located two blocks from the beach and three block from the bike path.

*****

I turned down my street and pulled into my driveway. For the next couple of hours, I was in my home office and back aboard the computer, engrossed in my latest appraisal project. A little after 11:00 a.m., it was time to meet Marti for breakfast. Fifteen minutes later, I pulled into the restaurant's parking lot. Twenty minutes late is just on time, I always say. Marti's car was nowhere in sight.

After taking my seat in the cafe, I read through the menu to pass a little time. By no means am I a creature of habit, but the only two items I've ever ordered are so good I can't get past them to try anything else.

Someone had left their copy of the Petoskey Daily News on a nearby table and I snagged it, knowing it might be a while longer before Marti showed up. Today's headline announced more lay-offs at local manufacturing companies. After skimming the article, I turned to page two. I was perusing that headline as Marti showed up, about 30 minutes late, explaining, "Hi, Onalee. I'm on appraiser time today."

"No problem," I said, understanding completely. Marti was dressed in a pale blue and yellow checked shirt and faded jeans. I guess she could be described as short, but she is so vibrant she fills up a lot of space. Sitting down, she grabbed a menu.

"You getting the usual?"

"Yes," I said as the waitress brought us coffee and took our orders.

"You been busy?" Marti asked between sips.

"Pretty much. But not swamped."

"Same with me. Hey, look at this," Marti said after she flipped open another section of the paper "Eco Terrorism Suspected in Arson Fire at Petoskey Condos."

"Really? Which project?"

"Let's see. Okay, it says it's called Whispering Pines."

"Oh my gosh." I yelped. I had appraised that thing. "You know, that property has been a fiasco from day one. In fact, remember last fall when you were up here visiting me and we sashayed around looking at the fall colors?"

She smiled. "Oh yes. It was gorgeous. I thought about dropping everything down there and moving up here."

"You should, like I keep telling you," I said and savored another sip of coffee. "Anyway, that day we drove right through the valley where they built this condo project but they hadn't broken ground yet. Actually, it's just west of Potato Soup Valley. Do you remember that area?"

"Hmmm," she said, frowning slightly trying to remember.

"It's a few miles down the road from that party store where we stopped to buy our sacks of chocolate covered black licorice."

"Oh yeah. Now, I remember," she said, smiling with the remembrance of sugars past.

"That area was so pretty. And so pristine. It seemed like there was nothing but hills and forests for miles."

"I know. The few homeowners who did live around there had bought their properties thinking they would be able to enjoy the quiet countryside. Then, along come some developers, and all of a sudden a small city is springing up on their doorsteps."

"Urban sprawl strikes again."

"Exactly," I said, warming to one of my favorite subjects, the ongoing loss of wilderness areas. Just then, the waitress set down two steaming dishes of crepes and poured both of us more coffee.

After several bites, I summed it up, "A coalition of homeowners, the township and environmentalists fought against the project for months. But as usual, they lost. How're your crepes?"

"Yum." Marti tended to be succinct when a plate of food was in front of her.

*****

After our meal, Marti left for her home in Metro Detroit and I motored back to my house. I called a few more brokers before turning on my computer. Janine from Fourth Financial Bank had emailed me. The crazy thing was that it was about Whispering Pines.

Chapter Two

Apparently, construction of the first phase of the condos was complete, and the bank needed me to go back out and check that it had been finished according to the plans.

I called Janine and got the go-ahead to do this construction draw analysis. These deals are relatively quick, easy and good money so for once I wouldn't be on appraiser time.

* * * * *

"Hi, this is Onalee O'Conner calling for Jonathon Richmond," I said, hoping I could get started right away on Whispering Pines. As I waited to be connected, I pictured Jonathon, one of two developers of the project. He was a good looking guy. I think he was somewhere in his late 40s, between five and ten years older than me, and his dark hair was streaked with gray. I'd never seen him in anything but expensive suits that looked great on his lean frame.

There were always stories about him with various women, other than his wife, and I suspected that they were true. Then again, it has been hard for me to cut a guy any slack these days. Actually, I'm totally slackless since my break up with the low down womanizer now known as the "Odious Tim".

He came on the line. "Hi Jonathon, this is Onalee O'Conner. The bank wants me to come out to your development and do the construction draw analysis. But, I need to ask you, was there much damage done by the fire?"

"Hi Onalee. How are you?" His voice sounded warm as always. "And to answer your question, no. A guy driving by saw the flames and called 9-1-1 on his cell. Lucky for us, the fire truck was already in the area, responding to a small brush fire. They were able to get there right away and put the fire out before much damage was done. Thank God no one was hurt."

"That's for sure," I said.

"I just hope they catch the crackpot who did it. Anyway, I can meet you at the model tomorrow at 3:00 if that's okay with you."

"That's fine. See you then." I worked on the industrial building for a couple of more hours, and then stepped into the kitchen to prepare one of my favorite dinners, a king-size tub of popcorn. My stovetop popper has seen better days and the stirring rod no longer stirs. But that's what we were given hands for, to shake popcorn poppers.

Hot Property

The following morning, Tuesday, I was rising and shining at the merry old hour of 4:45, a.m. thanks to a real estate broker I knew named Rick Sommers. I needed to ask him about a couple of industrial buildings he'd sold just north of Detroit in Auburn Hills. Occasionally, I appraise buildings around Detroit. I do this mainly in order to see Marti and to get a meal or two of Indian food. I got my questions answered, fit in a bit of flirting, masquerading as witty repartee and was showered and dressed by 5:30. After a couple of cups of coffee, I walked around opening windows just a crack to let in the fresh but cool June wind. Then I flopped in front of my computer and worked on my appraisal. About 2:50, I changed out of my un-dressy casual wear and into a black knit tee shirt, black slacks and pink silk suit jacket. Clunky low heels and trouser socks completed my ensemble.

It was just after 3:00 as I galloped down the front stairs and slid in behind my steering wheel. Since we were having a typical northern Michigan early June afternoon, I wasn't any too hot with my light suit jacket on. A stiff westerly wind was sending fluffy white clouds scudding across the sky. It had been dry around here for weeks and unfortunately for the thirsty earth, no rain was riding about in these clouds, either.

I live on the north end of town so it was only a thirty to forty minute drive to Whispering Pines. Today, the pines along the entrance drive were bobbing and weaving in the wind. I drove past the large boulders spaced intermittently along the drive that are part of every upscale development these days.

The only car in the main parking lot as I pulled in was the Cadillac Escalade that I remembered belonging to Jonathon Richmond. It looked like the marketing staff had the day off.

The sour smell of burned wood wafted through my open window. One of the units to the far west was blackened along its sidewall and there was a gaping hole in the roof. Other than the unit with the fire damage, the project looked complete, at least on the exterior. I gathered up my camera, yellow legal pad and pencil and hurried towards the model. The door was ajar. I pushed it open and found myself in a living room set up as a temporary sales office. There was no sign of anyone.

"Hello? Jonathon? It's Onalee O'Conner," I said to the adjacent wall. My watch showed 3:14, well within the bounds of reasonable appraiser time. I waited for a few minutes but when he didn't show, I decided to start my walk-through of the model.

Hot Property

The living room was a large great-room with cathedral ceilings. One wall was painted in an attractive, deep grayish blue color. A sofa and several chairs were grouped around a low coffee table.

The kitchen was off to the left and featured upscale appliances and granite counters. When you've seen one of these properties you've seen them all, I thought. I breezed through the kitchen and headed for the bedroom wing. Two average sized bedrooms, and a bath, all decorated in designer colors were located along the rear wall of the unit.

The master bedroom suite took up the entire other side of this wing. I jotted a few notes, snapped another picture and then strode to the master bedroom. The door was closed. I pushed it open and there, right in front of me, in his elegant, designer suit, was Jonathon Richmond sprawled on the floor.

That blood-stain might never come out of that expensive Persian rug, perversely flashed through my mind as I heard myself scream. I turned around and stumbled out of the condo, gasping for air and trying to get rid of the smell of blood clinging to me. I tore open my car door, jumped in and hit the automatic door lock.

Chapter Three

I needed to call the police, pronto. I peeled out of the parking lot, racing past the row of trees, their branches clawing at the sky, and out to the main road. A party store was just a few miles away and at least there'd be people around.

A few minutes later, I wheeled into the parking lot, pulled out my cell phone, and punched in 9-1-1. I told the dispatcher what had happened and gave him my name and home phone number. Then, still in a daze, I stumbled inside the store and bought a bottle of water.

I couldn't stop shaking. I climbed back in my car and went over and over the scene in my mind. It was definitely Jonathon Richmond lying there and he was definitely dead. His eyes were wide open, and the blood on his chest probably meant that he had been murdered. I hadn't seen anyone or heard anything so it must've happened before I got there.

After a few minutes I heard the wail of sirens and saw police cars and an ambulance race by. I lingered awhile longer but I was feeling fidgety and at loose ends. I started the car and turned back down the road toward Whispering Pines.

The pulsating lights of the police cars and ambulance were visible from the main road. An officer was wrapping the area with yellow crime tape as I pulled up the drive. I parked at the rear of the parking lot but stayed in my car, observing the police walking around, and tramping in and out of the condo. It didn't take long for one of them to notice a civilian car under the trees. The officer, looking all of eighteen years old, strode over, leaned down and peered into my window.

"Hello, ma'am. You need to move on," he said.

"Hi. Well, um, I was the one who found the body and called 9-1-1," I said my voice sounding unsteady.

"Oh really." He pulled out a notebook. "We'll want to question you then. What's your name and phone number?"

I answered him and then asked, "Can you tell me anything? It looked like he was shot. Was he?"

"We don't know anything yet. Hang on," he said as he hurried over by the front door of the condo to talk to another man. They both glanced over in my direction and then walked back to my car. The other policeman was dressed in khaki slacks and a short-sleeved shirt. He was attractive looking in a Green Beret sort of way. "Ma'am, this is Detective Costas. He'd like to ask you a few questions." Meanwhile, the Detective had also taken a pad out of his pocket.

"Let's start from the beginning," said Mr. No-nonsense Costas. "Why did you come here this afternoon?"

"I'm an appraiser and I was checking on the completion of the first phase of construction of this project for the bank," I said stiffly.

"Did anyone know you were coming?"

"Yes, I was supposed to meet Mr. Richmond."

"When?"

"Three o'clock." I watched him scribble this down.

"We didn't receive a call from 9-1-1 until 3:24. Why is that?" He shot back.

Feeling a bit of heat creep into my face, I said, "Well, I got here a bit late. Since Mr. Richmond wasn't in the office I started walking around, taking a few notes."

He fixed his eyes on me. "Walking around? Where did you go?"

I retraced my route for him and then he said, "Did you see anything unusual?"

"Not until I got to the master bedroom and found the body."

"Tell me exactly what you saw."

I told him, then he asked, "Did you touch anything or move anything?"

"No. I know you're not supposed to do that."

"Good. How did you know he was dead?"

"Um. His eyes were wide open. . . I could just tell."

"Did you see anybody else, in the condo?"

"No."

"How about outside when you drove up?"

"No. . . . Holy mother of pearl! You think the murderer might have been in there while I was walking around, don't you?"

Ignoring my outburst, he continued, "What cars were here when you arrived?"

"Just Mr. Richmond's."

Again, his eyes bored into me. I noticed they were a watery cold blue. "How well did you know him?"

"I've known him for years but only because I appraised some of his properties, so I didn't know him well."

"Okay. Thanks Miss O'Conner. I may have more questions in the next few days. Stick around town," he said as he started to walk away.

I called after him, "Detective. Wait. What do you think happened?"

"Thanks, Miss O'Conner," he repeated. "You're free to go now." He strode back to the condo and went inside.

I sat there looking across the parking lot as policemen entered and left, all of them ignoring me. Finally, I turned the ignition key and slunk away to my home.

Chapter Four

The following morning I woke up a little after 8:00. Even though I'd slept in, I felt groggy and filled with dread. It had been hours before I'd finally dropped off to sleep. I pulled on my bike shorts and a tee shirt, then laced up my running shoes.

I always walk for about a block and ease into my jog. I rounded the corner at Lakeview moving towards the water. Normally I run up to the main parking lot of the county park and follow the bike path back the mile and a half to my house. Not today. I wanted to avoid shadowy areas beneath the trees. Besides, I craved the summery sound of gentle blue waters lapping the beach. I plodded along the lake's edge, skirting a few shore-walkers as I went. Even at this hour, the sun poured down on the sand and the shallows. Today would be a hot one. Unusual for June and it looked like our dry spell wasn't going to end anytime soon.

After my run and a shower, my head felt clearer. I called the bank about the appraisal. Needless to say, Janine was shocked when I related my story. She said she'd get back to me after discussing it with her supervisor. Then I called Marti to fill her in on my unusual inspection.

"Do you have any idea who did it?" she asked.

"No. Not unless it was the same person who started the fire."

"When do you think it happened?"

"I don't know."

"Was the vic cold? Had rigor mortis set in?" Marti reads even more detective novels than I do. "Did you touch the body?"

"No, I didn't touch anything and I don't know about any rigor mortis or body temperatures."

"No need to get snippy. Hmmn. You think the murderer was still around while you were there?"

"Don't say that, it's too creepy."

"Well, let's think about this. Who else could be a suspect?" she persisted.

"I don't know. Maybe half of Northern Michigan."

"On, this is a once in a lifetime opportunity to put all of your sleuthing skills to work. If that isn't reason enough for you to approach this with enthusiasm, just remember, she who finds the body is high up on the list of suspects. You need to get cracking and figure out who the real killer is so the heat will be off you."

$$\star\,\star\,\star\,\star\,\star$$

Later that day I heard from Janine again. "Onalee. We're still going to need your analysis on Whispering Pines. Of course, under the circumstances we can give you a little more time. When do you think you can finish it?"

"Actually, I don't know. I'll have to ask the police when I can go back out there." Don't they always say that the murderer returns to the scene of the crime? "I'll check with them and get right back to you, Janine," I hoped my voice sounded sincere.

The truth was that I felt torn. All of the detectives I've read about would be jumping at the chance for an invitation to search the crime scene. I've got to be honest, the thought of going back into that blood soaked boudoir was unappealing at best. Then add in a soupçon of sheer terror at the prospect of that ever-returning-to-the-scene slayer and you've got yourself the makings of one reluctant appraiser/sleuth.

I finally called the police station around 4:00 p.m., and was connected with Detective Costas. "Ah, the appraiser. I was going to call you. Who else knew that Mr. Richmond was meeting you at the condo?"

21

I thought for a minute, "I don't know. I think he might have been in the reception area of his office when we set it up because I could hear other people in the background. I imagine that the receptionist and some of the sales people might have known."

He grilled me for a few more minutes then gave permission to go back out to the model. The police had finished their investigation of the condo. Unfortunately, I didn't hear an offer to send any officers with me.

"Is it true that the murderer always goes back to the scene of the crime?" I asked with a voice held steady through sheer concentration.

"That's what they always say, don't they. Let me know if you see anyone suspicious."

"Yeah, thanks," I said feeling my lip curl down as I hung up.

I then called the R & L Land Company and asked to speak with Mike Lorian, the other half of R & L. I expressed my condolences about his partner, Jonathon, and then told him I needed to complete my inspection.

"Thanks, Onalee. Frankly, we're all in a state of shock. What a loss this is. Not just to the firm but to all of us, personally. Jon's funeral is tomorrow. The office will be closed all day and I'm not planning anything else. But, if you want, I could meet you out there the following day. That is, if you work on Saturdays. I assume this won't take too long."

"Thanks for fitting me in. Saturday would be fine." We arranged to meet at 11:00 a.m.

After hanging up, I decided that I needed to make another early morning phone call to my favorite broker. I wrote myself a note for the following day. It was now getting close to 5:00 and my yogurt and bran cereal luncheon were a distant memory. Two nights of popcorn dinners in one week, though not unheard of, might be a smidgeon unhealthy.

As I pondered, my thoughts turned to pizza. If I started now, I could have dinner made within the hour for tonight and the next four or five days. Digging out my Dad's trusty recipe, I began. I've used this recipe often enough that I could get in a little phoning while I worked.

"Marti. Guess what. I have to go back out to Whispering Pines."

"That's perfect. But aren't you nervous?" I heard her throaty little chuckle.

"Well, yeah." I said whacking the dough with my fist.

"When are you going?"

"Saturday. Richmond's funeral is tomorrow so his office is closed."

"You're going aren't you?"

"Where?" I asked.

"Duh. To the funeral. Maybe you're not big on funerals but all of those woman detectives go to them whenever someone is murdered."

"I know. That's always kind of bugged me about those stories," I said, not liking where this conversation was heading.

"Well, if they all go then you've got to. You're bound to learn something. Keep a sharp eye out, the murderer is always among the mourners."

"Marti. . . ."

"Go. And call me afterwards. This is getting juicy."

She hung up and I stretched and worked the dough out on a pizza stone. Then, I dumped a can of tomato paste in a bowl, threw in some oregano, garlic powder, salt and pepper, and using my favorite big wooden spoon, started stirring. Somehow, thick crimson sauce didn't look enticing today.

Bang! I jumped and my head jerked around towards the noise, the spoon clattering to the floor. Tomato sauce splashed on the cabinet and down the front of my shorts as a jolt of fear shot down my legs and deep into my toes. My heart was pounding like a jack-hammer. Then I spotted the culprit. A bird had flown into the window overlooking my backyard and now sat, head cocked to one side, dazed.

It didn't matter that it was still broad daylight, I scurried to the front door and secured the dead bolt. The bird was gone when I got back. I shivered, despite the heat pouring through the window from the late afternoon sun.

Just then, the doorbell rang. I grabbed a small paring knife that was on the counter. Just in case. Slowly, I made my way to the door. The chimes sounded again before I reached it. Looking through the peep hole, I observed Detective Costas standing on my porch.

"Hello Detective," I said, after opening the door for him.

"Ms. O'Conner?" His eyes strayed to my hand, then my leg. "I wouldn't mind if you put that knife down before you slash your other leg."

Oh my gosh. I'd forgotten the knife just like I forgot the pizza sauce. "Sorry," I said, trying to regain a modicum of composure. "I guess I'm still a little jumpy. Come in."

The Detective entered and we stood facing each other just inside the doorway. I didn't care to ask His Rudeness to sit and take his ease in my parlor. Instead, I blocked him from further entry into my house and, hopefully, into my life. He pulled his pad out and began questioning me again about details surrounding my discovery of Jonathon Richmond.

He started out in a civil manner but then became more and more hostile. At times, he gazed pointedly at my sauce-smeared shorts, just as a power play, or so it seemed. Frankly, I was growing weary of his harassment and determined to oppose it. Besides, it was time for some of my own concerns to be addressed.

"Detective," I asked, during a slight pause in the cross fire, "You're with the Petoskey police, aren't you?"

"Yes I am."

"Then why are you investigating a crime in the township?"

He sighed. "I'm deputized by the county. Because of scarce resources, I assist them with their violent crimes."

"Oh. Have you managed to locate the murder weapon?"

"Perhaps. Perhaps not. It's really not a matter of public knowledge."

"That may be true, but you've been grilling me as if I'm the murderer. If I am a suspect, I'm not just the 'general public' and I have the right to know."

"You are most definitely a suspect, Ms. O'Conner. But, the only right you have is to remain silent. I suggest it's time you exercise it. Good day," he said, as he turned and let himself out the door.

*****

Later that evening, my phone rang. I recognized the number of my good friend, Rosie Ryder.

"Hi, Rosie."

"We must be having a doozie of a cold summer, Onalee, because hell has definitely frozen over."

Chapter Five

"Pardon me? Has there been a big freeze down below?"

"Burt, my fiancé . . ."

"Your what?"

She continued in a cool voice, "Are you going to keep interrupting me, Onalee? My word. As I was saying, Burt and I would like you to be in our wedding."

"Yay, yay, yay! I can't believe it. This is so fantastic. I love Burt."

"Well, keep your mitts off my man. Besides, he's too old for you."

"I don't know about that, but, Rosie, come on. Give me details."

She giggled. "It happened last evening. We went out to dinner at our favorite place, that Chinese buffet over on State Street. Then he took me around to his place. We walked out behind the house, hand in hand. He said he wanted to show me his new flowers. Onalee, you know how I love marigolds? He'd planted yellow marigolds in a group of orange ones and they spelled out, 'Will U marry me?'

"It took me awhile to make it out and then I'm sure I gasped. I looked over and Burt was on one knee looking up at me and holding one marigold and a ring. I was crying and laughing all at once. Of course I said yes."

I wiped away the tears streaming down my own cheeks. "Oh, Rosie, that is so romantic."

"I know. Imagine at our ages."

"What do you mean? You two can outdo most people half your age."

"Oh, hush, Onalee. Anyway, what do you say? Will you or won't you be in our wedding?"

"Abso-posi-tutely. I'd love to."

"Great. The date is going to be June 25th, it's a Saturday. Put it on your calendar."

"This summer?"

"Yup. We don't want to wait. Can you make it?"

"Rosie, that's just a few weeks from now. Can you get everything organized in time? What can I do to help?"

"Nothing, but thanks, Onalee. We're keeping it simple. I'm looking at gowns for all of you attendants right now. I want to find dresses that you'll all be able to wear again." She said and paused for effect then burst out laughing.

I chuckled to keep her company but I had an uneasy feeling about this. Her ensembles were legendary among our friends. "Just remember, Rosie. Go easy on us. I may get married myself someday and you know I'm not above exacting a grisly bit of revenge."

We talked a little more about the upcoming nuptials and then moved on to a discussion about Rosie's "kids". She taught badminton to a group of young players at a rec center in her hometown of Flint. Apparently a couple of them were showing real promise and she was planning to take them to a tournament near Detroit. Then we caught up on mutual chums from the world of badminton. I told her a bit about finding the body, she cautioned me to be careful, we shared a couple more laughs and signed off.

I thought about the happy couple as I got ready for bed. Rosie and Burt, both in their early eighties, had met on a badminton court years ago and become mixed doubles partners as well as great friends. Burt was married at that time and his wife, Brenda and Rosie also had hit it off. Several years ago, Brenda contracted cancer and died. A year or so after that, Burt asked Rosie out to dinner and now Rosie was on her way to blushing bride-dom for the first time in her life.

Hot Property

* * * * *

Friday Morning—4:45 a.m.

I awakened and hurried through my vocal warm-ups. I hoped to eliminate any early morning raspiness. Then, if all went according to plan, only melodious, jewel tones would spring forth to fall as gently as an early summer rain on the eager ears of Mr. Sommers. I placed my call.

"Onalee, how are you," Rick was talking on his speaker phone.

"Good. You?"

"Great, but is everything really okay?"

"Um yeah. I think so," I said not wanting to talk about the murder right then. "Anyway I need to ask you about a few more buildings."

He rattled off facts about recent sales and leases of industrial buildings while I scribbled down notes. "Any questions?"

"Um no. I think I'm all set."

"Then I've got one for you. Is it true that you found Jonathon Richmond's body?" His voice sounded more intimate now that he had switched off the speaker phone.

"How'd you hear about that?" I squeaked.

"So, it is true. I heard it through the real estate grapevine. Tell me about it."

I filled him in on the main parts, glossing over the details in case they weren't public knowledge.

"Did you know him?" I asked.

"Oh sure. You knew he started out down here, in metro Detroit, didn't you?"

"Yeah, I did. What did you think of him?"

"He was a pretty decent guy." He lowered his voice, "A real skirt chaser though. I'll bet he came on to you didn't he?"

"Well. . . he kind of did, I guess, but I kept him at arm's length. I sure wasn't interested. Everybody knew he was married," I said. "Who do you think did it?"

"I could think of a bunch of people. A number of planning board members, especially up in your neck of the woods. Jealous husbands. Maybe his partner. His wife.

Jealous girlfriends. And of course, the person who discovers the body is always a prime suspect, isn't she?"

"Very funny, especially at 4:50 in the morning."

"Hey, when are you coming back down here? I think we should go to lunch."

"You sure you want to risk that," I said, in my silkiest sultriest tone.

"I could take you in a fair fight, so, yes."

"Um, I don't know when I'll be there, but it sounds like fun."

"Next week," he persisted.

"Well maybe. I just don't know yet."

"Okay. I'll call you Monday. Bye."

"Rick." I was talking to a dial tone. I sure hoped he didn't call on Monday at 4:45 a.m.

* * * * *

Later that morning, I got a call from Marti, reminding me of my obligations to the amateur sleuth sisterhood.

"Especially since you're a prime suspect, you need to go to the funeral."

So, grumbling to myself, I dressed in a gray business suit and drove to the funeral home. I wondered if there would be much of a turn-out. He was despised in some circles, but there were actually quite a few people in attendance.

I was running a little late and was forced to slip in to a seat in the rear of the funeral home. This turned out to be a brilliant plan because it allowed me to surreptitiously check everyone out. I glanced around, disbelief growing as I noted pewful

33

after pewful of glitteringly glamorous ladies. Had I slipped into some alternate universe? Makes you wonder how many babes were bedded by Jonathon. How had he ever found time to fit in any developing?

The whole staff of the R & L Land Company was clustered together near the front. I recognized his partner, Mike Lorian, who was staring straight ahead at the casket, his arm loosely draped around the woman on his right. Another lady, dabbing at her eyes with a tissue, was on his left. She had shoulder length brown hair cut in a classic pageboy, the preferred hairstyle of the Michigan old money set.

The service hadn't started yet and some of the other people from his office spoke quietly to each other. I knew several of the sales people.

As my primary reason for being here was to detect, my roving eyes slid off that group to continue their rounds and smashed right into the ice blue eyes of Detective Costas. My head snapped forward, as my cheeks lit up and the reverend began to speak. I definitely needed to go back and study some of my old mystery novels. I'd completely forgotten that the police also attend these funerals.

An hour or so later, I was threading through the somber group of people leaving the service.

Hot Property

"I thought you didn't know Mr. Richmond very well, Miz O'Conner." The flat voice of Detective Costas emanated from close behind my left elbow.

I turned partly around, "Um, no I didn't. But I feel sort of connected now, as you can imagine." He treated me to another of his penetrating looks before I was, mercifully, carried away from him by the departing crowd.

Exiting the parking lot, I looked back and saw Costas standing near the front walkway. He was staring at Mike Lorian and the woman he'd had his arm around in the service. She was tall and thin with silvery blond hair. They both looked grim. Cars were lining up behind me, so I tore my eyes off the rear view mirror and wheeled out into traffic.

After reaching my house, I quickly changed out of my suit and into my summer uniform of shorts, a tee shirt, and flip-flops. Today, orange flips were selected to pick up an orange stripe in my tee shirt. I then got down to work on the industrial building.

There was only one phone call that day and that was from Marti needing a post funereal update. After that, I worked until dinnertime and then reheated two slices of O'Conner pizza. After dinner I hopped back on the computer for a few more hours than dug out an old mystery novel. Leafing through, I read about a heroine facing extreme danger while being relentlessly hassled by the police for what they unfairly perceived as interference. Well, I wouldn't meddle, I decided, though I might lend a bit of a hand if called upon. After that, I double-checked that the front door and door to my deck were secured and went to bed.

* * * * *

Saturday morning I got up with my alarm at 6:00 a.m. and headed out the door for my run. It was cool but felt like it was, once again, going to sizzle. Oh, how we needed some rain. On a personal level, I love the preternaturally hot, dry days we are experiencing because of global warming. But, I hate the toll it is exacting on the world and my beautiful little corner of it.

After a shower and my breakfast of two graham crackers and tea I started back to work. About 9:00 I got a call from Mike Lorian asking me to meet him at the office to ride out to the model with him. Remembering that Rick had mentioned him as a possible suspect, I said, "Mike, I've got to be out and about all morning. Why don't I just meet you there?"

"Nonsense. This way, if there are any questions, you can ask me then. I think it'll save us both time."

It might be an opportunity to learn something, I thought. And if the office staff knew I was going there with Mike he wouldn't dare try anything. Would he?

"Okay."

"See you at 11:00 then."

Chapter Six

At about twenty to eleven, I hopped in my car
and drove over to R and L. Ten minutes early
is just on time is my new motto. Actually, I
wanted to hang around the office to see if I
could pick up on any unusual dynamics among
the staff, meanwhile making sure everyone knew
that I was going to be at the crime scene with
Mike Lorian.

At R and L, the receptionist informed me
that Mike had stepped out. "I'll wait," I
said, to the pretty, dark haired girl behind
the desk. "I'm a little early, anyway."
Clearly not interested, she went back to
whatever she was typing on the computer. How
can anyone type with inch long nails? They
looked professionally painted and manicured.
Didn't I hear that those treatments usually
cost about forty dollars a crack? And her
clothes didn't look like JC Penee to this
little fashion cognoscente. I felt my eyes

narrow in speculation. Does R and L pay their receptionists big bucks or was I looking at a possible kept woman/suspect?

"Is there anyone here that could answer some questions about Whispering Pines?" I asked, interrupting her work flow.

She eyed me coolly, "Can I ask what this is regarding?"

"Sure. I need to re-appraise it for the bank." I flashed her a grin.

She sighed, then punched a few numbers into her phone and announced my presence to someone in the back offices. The door opened and a tall, willowy woman strode towards me and handed me her card. She was the most beautiful person, I think I had ever seen in real life.

"Hi." Her smile sparkled. "I'm Marissa Martin, marketing director for R and L. Follow me and we'll talk."

Her office was nicely appointed with a light oak desk and comfortable chairs. A window framed a view of pine trees interspersed with feeding stations. Birds flitted in and out of view and pecked at seeds on the ground and in the feeders.

Following my glance, Marissa said, "Whatever project we develop, we try to do in harmony with nature and the environment. It costs us a lot more money, but the funny thing is. . ." She paused for a smile break. "I'll bet it's actually paid for itself in customer satisfaction and good PR. Environmentalists love us," she said, again smiling.

"Well, maybe not all environmentalists."

Her grin faded and she gave me a hard look. "I don't think you can call the person who set the fire at Whispering Pines an environmentalist. More like an eco- terrorist or nutcase."

"Mike Lorian thinks the arsonist may be the one who killed Jonathon Richmond."

After giving me another piercing look, she said, "Wait a minute, are you the appraiser, um . . ."

"Who found his body? Yes."

"Oh. Oh my gosh." she said her eyes widening. "That's terrible."

I eased into one of the cushy looking chairs as she sat down behind her desk. "You worked with him, who do you think did it?"

"Boy. I don't know." She stared out the window for a bit then turned back, "He did have his share of enemies."

"Like who?"

"Well, I'm sure you've heard the gossip. There's a list of old girlfriends, a mile long, including just about everyone but yours truly. . . jealous husbands. . . and of course, Janet, his wife.

"So he really did play the field."

"Oh, come on. He must have hit on you," she said, flashing me a wide grin.

"Kind of," I said. "But I was pretty involved at the time and I don't think he tried too hard. Why not you?"

She sighed. "We'd been friends for forever and I knew his pattern. If I'd let him, he would have loved me enough to be as faithful to me as he had been to his gazillion and five other girlfriends." She shook her head. "I couldn't deal with that and stay friends. And, I wanted to stay friends. Don't get me wrong. He tried. But we talked about it and both decided, nope, don't want to go there."

"He sounds even worse than the last guy I was unfortunately involved with. Why are some guys like that?"

Her laugh was musical. "If I knew that, I'd write a book and make a ton of money."

"They'd probably give you the Nobel Peace Prize or something." That brought out another chuckle from her. "Who was his latest squeeze?"

"You mean squeeze-es? There's always one or two. Plus, his wife of course." She leaned closer and lowered her voice. "Believe it or not, he and Linda Lorian, you know, his partner's wife? They'd been keeping time lately. And, if you think that Secretary Susie, out front, was hired for her brains and typing abilities, then I'll definitely have a ton of appraisal work for you. And of course I'll expect nice sky-high values on everything."

I felt her eyes on me as I sat there, stunned. His partner and best friend's wife. The man had no moral boundaries. "Wow," I squeaked. "Did Mike know about that? I mean the deal with his wife?" I'd liked Jonathon but how could he have been so disgusting?

"Hmmm. I don't think guys spot this stuff like we do. But everyone else in the office knew it, so maybe." She paused and seemed to be thinking that over. Then nodding her head she said, "Yes. I think he knew."

"Why do you stay at R and L?"

"Because of the money. Where else can I find a great paying job in northern Michigan? And I do love it up here." She gazed out the window for a moment then turned back to me and continued, "The other thing is, I can do my job and not really have that much involvement with either Mike or Jonathon. Anyway, you had questions about Whispering Pines?"

We talked about the project for a few minutes then the receptionist, who might be named Susie, let us know that Mike was waiting in the lobby.

We both stood up, "Are you afraid to ride out there with him?" She asked almost in a whisper.

I stopped walking and turned back towards her, "Should I be?"

"Well, he knows that we all know you're with him so I wouldn't think he'd try anything. Besides, he probably isn't the killer."

"Why don't you think he's the killer?"

"Oh, I really have no idea. I just said that so you'd be less scared. I'm sure it's safe," she snickered again, but this time she laughed alone.

Chapter Seven

"Sorry I'm late, Onalee," Mike said, holding the front door open for me.

"No problem, except that I did tell Janine at the bank that I'd call her this afternoon after you and I went out to Whispering Pines."

"A banker working on a Saturday. I'm impressed."

Oops, I'd forgotten that teensy detail.

"Anyway, it's only 11:15 now and we should be back by 12:30 or 1:00. I think you'll be able to squeeze a call in before the end of the day."

I heard a snicker and saw that Marissa had followed me out and was trying to catch my eye. I spun on my heel and marched out the door, behind Mike.

We got in his car, a BMW convertible, and he nosed it into traffic. We talked about the weather and the play-offs; the Redwings were close to winning the Stanley cup again, and other innocuous topics. As we turned onto Whispering Pines Drive and headed towards the condos, Mike fell silent. Glancing over at him, I saw that his face had hardened and he was staring straight ahead. He parked the car and we climbed out.

"I'll need to also inspect the fire-damaged unit," I said, shattering the silence.

"Sure. We can go in any of the units you want. Let's go into that one first." His left eye was twitching.

Inside, there was smoke and water damage but it wasn't as bad as I'd thought. Mike gave me an estimate on the cost to repair it. I took some notes and a few pictures and we quickly left the acrid interior and stepped back into the fresh summer air. Emerging from the heavy quiet of the burned unit, the day felt glorious. Birds were singing even though I hadn't noticed them before.

We walked through the rest of the project and I measured the exterior walls. It was basically complete except for the finishing touches that would be chosen by future buyers. The model was the last thing we had to see before we could leave. Mike opened the door and looked back at me. His left eye was really jumping, now. Why was he so nervous? I stepped through the door and into the unit, being careful to stay behind him.

We meandered through the living room, the kitchen and then the two smaller bedrooms just as I'd done on Wednesday. The door to the master bedroom was, just as before, closed. Mike reached for the doorknob then spun around. Adrenaline shot through me and I jumped away from him.

"Sorry," he said. "I didn't mean to startle you. I haven't been out here since . . . since before Jon was killed. This gives me the creeps."

"Me too," I squeaked. Then we were standing just inside the door, staring at the stained Persian rug in front of us, acting as a barrier to the rest of the room. Mike stepped around it with me on his heels. I thought I ought to at least look around on the other side of the bed, although it didn't seem likely that the police would have missed anything. Also, I needed to poke my head into the master bath situated on the far side of the room. Nothing looked out of place and if the cops had missed anything, then I did too.

Outside again, Mike locked the door and we walked towards his car. Although there was a wide expanse of lawn and parking lot in front of the building, the woods hugged the sides and rear. Had someone quietly slid open the bedroom window, climbed out and ducked behind a tree last Wednesday? Had he or she watched as I found the body, screamed and rushed outside? I shivered, but thinking back on it, the only cars in the parking lot had belonged to me and to Jonathon.

Mike was looking at me searchingly. "What happened when you found Jonathon?"

Ignoring his fluttering left eye, I filled him in using generalities and not revealing any details.

He leaned in closer and dropped his voice, "Did you see anybody or hear anything?"

"No." I said, stepping back from him. I hoped like heck he believed me. He gave me a long look, then abruptly opened the car door. He wasn't the only one with burning questions but I thought I'd wait a bit to ask.

★★★★★

Mike was talking about his daughter and her high school tennis career as we reached the busy commercial area on the outskirts of Petoskey. "Sounds like she is a tough competitor, all right. Does she play singles or does she sometimes have a partner"

"She just plays singles."

"Oh. Speaking of partners," I said, ever the smooth seguer. Or is it segueist? "How did you and Jonathon hook up?"

"We were commercial brokers at Langdon and Marsh in Detroit. This was a long time ago. And, we were each putting together little developments. Four-unit apartments. Small retail buildings. All nickel and dime stuff. They usually needed work and we put in a lot of sweat equity." He glanced over at me. "You know, new drywall, paint. I even got to be a pretty fair plumber. Jonathon called this 'junior achievement stuff'.

"One day in the office, we were just sitting around, shooting the breeze, when it hit us that if we joined forces we could both get ahead a whole lot faster. And it worked great. We started getting involved in bigger and bigger things and, I guess, the rest is history."

"How did you guys get along?"

"Fine. I mean, of course we didn't always see eye to eye. But, actually, we usually did. And we were always able to work things out. He was such a visionary." He paused. "It's going to be tough without him."

"I'll bet," I said. Was this a carefully rehearsed script? At least the last few lines came off that way. Or was I just looking for things? It was time to go for it.

"I've heard so many stories about his affairs. Was that ever a problem between you two?"

He swung his head around to look at me, and then had to slam on the brakes as the car ahead abruptly slowed up. "Sorry," he said and trained his eyes back on the road. The eye that had quit twitching while he discussed his daughter, had resumed its fits and starts.

"Was it ever a problem?" I repeated.

"What? Oh. It wasn't cool. I mean I was never into that kind of thing. But, we usually worked around it. None of them ever lasted very long," he said and then in a low voice almost talking to himself, continued, "of course, then it was always on to the next."

"Wow. Did you usually know who he was seeing?"

"Uh, no. Like I said I wasn't interested. I tried to avoid the whole thing."

"Do you think it was one of his ex-girlfriends or a jealous husband that killed Jonathon?"

He scowled, "You mark my words. They're going to find it was the tree-hugger. You know, the guy who tried to burn down our building. Anyone who would do that has already proven that he's capable of murder, at least in my book," he said as he pivoted his car into a parking spot in front of R and L. He stopped the car but left it running. "Onalee, call if you need anything else for the appraisal."

"Okay and thanks," I said climbing out. The elegant Marissa was walking out the door as Mike drove off.

49

"Hello," she said, smiling. Glad to see you made it back safely. I'm on my way to lunch, want to go?"

"Sure, I'm starving." We took my car and wound up at my favorite coffee house. The smell of fresh roasted coffee permeated the air. Reading the menu on the chalk board, I was torn between their corn chowder and a Greek sandwich but the sandwich won. Marissa settled for the chowder. Since it was about 75 degrees, we took our lunches out on the deck overlooking Little Traverse Bay.

It was breezy and sailboats dotted the lapis-hued lake below us. We talked about our jobs for a while but the conversation inevitably turned to guys and the lack of them in northern Michigan. That is, for anybody over the age of 30. Then Marissa began talking about Jonathon. They'd met in Detroit years ago and had been friendly competitors at rival companies. Jonathon moved north but they'd kept in touch.

"One day we were talking on the phone and I guess I was whining about the long drive I'd have to take to get to a good beach and he said something like, why don't you move up here? I'll hire you. Why not, I thought. I could always move back if I didn't like it. So I did it. And I've never looked back."

"And have you met anyone since you've been up here?"

"Of course not. But, that may be my own fault. I put in tons of hours at work. What about you?"

Wowzer. If the most gorgeous woman in Northern Michigan couldn't find a man, we were all in trouble. "No. I put in a lot of hours too. Besides, I'm not sure it's possible. Unless, you count meeting guys over the internet."

I chewed and she sipped, my sandwich and her soup, in silence for a while. I was reflecting on the abysmal dating scene and Marissa's thoughts were probably similarly enmeshed.

"Mike missed his chance to off me," I said breaking into the quiet. "Do you think that means he didn't kill Jonathon, either?"

"Could be."

"Does his eye always twitch? I've never noticed it before but then I haven't been around him that much."

"Only when he's flustered. It was twitching today, I gather?"

"Like a Mexican jumping bean on espresso," I said.

"Really. That's odd," She said and toyed with her soup. There were a few moments of silence. Out on the bay, one of the sailboats had raised a crimson and blue spinnaker as it glided towards us.

I broke into her reverie, "Who else do you think is a likely candidate?"

She swallowed a spoonful of soup, "After all these years, Jon's wife Janet can't be the jealous type. My guess is that they've lived separate lives for a long time. That leaves Linda Lorian, the tree hugger," she was counting the suspects off on her fingers, "Possibly some of the township officials that got involved in the Whispering Pines zoning fiasco, old loves that we've never heard of, and, my personal favorite nominee, Susie Secretary."

"And, Mike Lorian," I added.

"Yes. And of course, you." She gave me an impish grin. "You did find the body, you know. I can see the headline now, Avenging Appraiser . . . Axes Ace. . . Ace. . . Ace Acreage Developer."

"Real funny."

"Sorry," she said, her grin fading. "But, I've just lost a guy who was one of my best friends. I've got to laugh or I'll cry. She gazed off into the distance for a moment. Then, as she regained her composure, she turned back to me. "Anyway, I've got to get going." With that, we both stood up, gathered our dishes and took them back inside the restaurant.

Later, at home I worked on the Whispering Pines update for a while and then called it a day.

On Sunday, I hit the beach with my few friends who are willing to risk skin cancer. The day was hot but the water was only about 50 degrees and not even the kids were swimming.

★★★★★

"Onalee, I found it." Rosie had called again.

"Great. I knew you would." Uh oh, I was afraid my short-term memory was going. "Now, um, what did you tell me you were missing?"

She laughed. "I guess I put the cart before the horse, didn't I? I found the perfect bridesmaids' dresses for you girls."

"You girls?" Rosie thinks everyone under the age of sixty is "just a kid". "Oh, wonderful," I said hoping I'd mustered up an excited edge to my voice.

"I need your dress size and, just to be on the safe side, your measurements."

"Now?"

"No time like the present," she declared.

"Okay. Give me a minute to hunt up a tape measure." I looked in three drawers but

53

couldn't find one. I'm not much of a seamstress but I thought I was equipped with the rudimentary materials of the craft.

"Onalee? Are you still there?"

"Yes, but can I get back to you?"

"I'd rather"

"Wait a sec. I just thought of something." I strode to my closet and pulled out my one hundred foot tape that I use for appraising. "Hang on, I've got to lay the phone down." I stretched out a length of the tape and sucking in, wrapped it around my waist. Oh dear. Wasn't Scarlet O'Hara's waist a mere 18 inches? Let's just say mine measured somewhere between Ms. O'Hara's and a fully inflated beach ball. I gave Rosie my less than ideal figure figures.

"Okay, I have everyone's now. I'm going to go ahead and order the dresses. I'll have yours sent right up to your house. Let me know the second you get it."

Chapter Eight

The following morning's sun found me up early and galvanizing into action. I ran and then worked on the industrial building for a bit. I also bid on a few other jobs. By late afternoon I finished my appraisal and sent it off to the bank. It would be a couple of days late, unless of course one went by appraiser time.

I was driving home from the post office in my usual post-deadline euphoria when I saw a strange car in my driveway. A wave of chills washed over me. I drove on by and circled the block hoping I could figure out who it was. But there, on my front porch, sat Marti waving and grinning. I backed up and pulled into the drive beside her sporty new car.

"Surprised to see me?"

"Ah, yeah. What are you doing here?"

"Boy, some welcome. I came to help on our investigation. Anything new by the way?"

"Shouldn't you be working? And there is no, 'our investigation.'"

As I sat down on the porch beside her she ignored my pleas for sanity and asked again to be brought up to speed on "the case" as she also referred to it. So I had no choice but to tell her everything that had happened in the last few days.

"What are you planning to do now?" she asked.

"Work on my next appraisal and let the police solve this 'case'"

"What?" she shrieked, glaring at me, "Come on now, the Onalee I know is always ready for an adventure and would never pass up a golden opportunity like this."

"Opportunity. Shmoportunity." I said petulantly. "This kind of 'adventure' can get us killed."

"Where's your sense of civic duty? If this killer is allowed to go Scott-free, innocent men, women and children all over Northern Michigan may be in danger. Not to mention the fact that this type of thing tears great holes in the fragile fabric of civilization." All the while she nodded her head, apparently in strong agreement with herself.

"Oh puleeze."

"Tell you what. If I can't appeal to your sense of honor or adventure, then I will insist that you exercise old fashioned good

56

manners. I'm your guest and you have to entertain me."

"What?"

"You heard me. And what I want to do first, is to revisit the crime scene. I've visualized it from your briefings but I need to actually see it."

Briefings. Give me a break. "The cops don't really like people messing up their work you know. And, it could be very dangerous."

"So you said," she said dismissively. "Give me a sec to put my bags inside and we'll go. There's still tons of daylight."

A few minutes later we were in my car driving north towards Whispering Pines. By the time we arrived, the model and all of the other units were locked for the night. Leaving the car, Marti strode over and looked in the few windows that didn't have their shades down. Standing in front of the model, she demanded a minute by minute account of what had happened from when I walked through the front door to the time I found Jonathon lying on the floor.

I was dealing with the heebie-jeebies again, not only because we were at the scene, but also reliving it by talking about it. A branch cracked somewhere close by and we both jumped and swiveled our heads around searching for the origin of the noise. Abruptly, a deer came into view around the corner of the building, saw us and froze. Then she turned and loped away, white tail held high.

"Wow. We don't usually get to see deer up close and personal in Detroit," Marti said, seemingly fully recovered. "Hey, let's go around in back and check out the woods. The killer might have frequented there at some point."

"Are you immune to the creeps?" I asked in a voice that sounded too shrill.

"Just ignore them," she said striding ahead of me. "If you indulge them, they'll never go away."

I followed her into the hardwoods. In the spring, the forest floor is laden with wildflowers of all colors. Lady's Slippers, like tiny yellow ballerina shoes bob among snowy white trillium and jack-in-the-pulpits. Now, in early June, we weren't likely to see much. Of course, Herlock Holmes there, wasn't interested in horticulture anyway. We traipsed hither and yon and farther and further, all the while getting scratched by wild blackberry brambles and finding nothing in the way of any clues.

"Aghghghg!" Marti screamed and raced back towards me, legs pumping high into the air as her toes skimmed the ground.

"What? Are you all right? What happened?" I shrieked.

"I almost stepped on a snake," she said as she passed by me.

"Gees. Is that all? You scared me."

"Well excuse me. I hate those things." She slowed to a walk but kept heading back towards the condos. I said a silent thank you to Mr. Serpent and followed her out.

By the time we reached the clearing in front of the building, it was about 8:00 p.m. and still daylight. Taking the lead now, I was opening the car door as Marti sauntered past, heading in the direction of the pines, along the drive. "Now where are you going?"

"We've got time. Let's see what's past these trees."

I sighed loudly but it was wasted on Marti, who was out of hearing range. Once again I tagged along behind her. Inside the forest it was easy walking with very little undergrowth.

"Doesn't it smell good in here?" Marti asked.

"Sure does," I said breathing in the tangy air. The pines eventually gave way to scattered hardwoods and scrub trees. Great, I would soon be able to add to my collection of abrasions.

I was beginning to feel a bit grumpy. This hostess stuff was for the birds. And besides, my guest had invited herself, so how much entertaining was I morally obligated to do? Marti walked on, oblivious to the seething and gnashing of teeth going on behind her. We eventually happened upon a clearing and there, bounding towards us was a gorgeous hunk of black and white dog.

"Caesar, come. Caesar . . . He's friendly." The dog galloped, tail wagging, first to Marti, then to me. He gazed up at me as I petted his big head. He had a "Glad to be alive," glint shining in his eyes.

"Hey, sorry." The man said coming closer, "He shouldn't run up to . . ." he was studying my face, "Onalee?"

I looked at Caesar's owner more closely. He was about medium height, with a trim build and sandy hair. He was attractive in an out doorsy way. "Frank? Hi. What are you doing here?"

"I live up there." he said pointing back towards a mammoth hill. What are you doing here?"

"It's kind of a long story," I said.

"Yes," Marti said, pushing in front of me, "But an interesting one. Especially for you, since you live in this neighborhood. She found a body just across the way there so now we're back at the crime scene searching for clues."

"Marti."

"Well, maybe he saw something, On. Hi, I'm Marti Gonzalez," she said displaying her best dimply grin.

Looking slightly thunderstruck, Frank shook her outstretched hand. Then, since it was my turn to be stricken, I heard him say, "As a matter of fact, I do know something. I guess I'm the number one arson suspect for the fire over there. And, apparently, that fact then qualified me to be high on the list of accused persons for the murder of Jonathon Richmond." He stopped and studied me. "Onalee? Are you okay?"

"Frank. You're kidding me. Right?" I asked.

He gave me a rueful grin. "I wish I was."

"So, because you're a neighbor. . . And you must have been one of the protesters against the condos," I said, trying to reason my way out of my dazed condition.

"Oh yes. I fought it big time. I was at every planning meeting. I circulated petitions. Met with all of the planners. We managed to delay the project but, as usual, money talked."

"Did you do it? Start the fire, I mean," Marti said, confronting him.

"No. Of course not. I mean, I can't say I'm sorry it happened, but, I'm not an eco-

61

terrorist," Frank said looking directly into Marti's eyes.

"What about Jonathon Richmond?" I asked.

"You mean did I knock him off? No, I'm also not a killer."

"Where were you on the afternoon he was killed?" I asked.

"I was here. I work out of my house quite a bit of the time. So, no, to answer your next question, Detective O'Conner, I don't have an alibi. That is, unless you'll take Caesar's word for it. Come to think of it though, he was probably lying in the sun asleep when it happened so I guess I could've snuck out and he wouldn't have known it, either."

"No need to get snippety," I said. "Did you hear anything or see anything?" We appraisers are more than comfortable with asking prying questions.

"Not a thing. At least not until I heard a bunch of sirens."

"When did the police haul you in?" Marti chimed in, double-teaming him.

He chuckled, obviously finding her abrupt manner endearing. "They didn't waste any time. The night of the fire they came banging on my door. They let me go right away, because they had nothing on me. Then Richmond gets killed." He shook his head, "Again, I'm not real broken up about it but I didn't do it. The upshot was that I got to spend even more time at the county jail getting grilled. I'd never been at a police station in my life, and then twice in one week."

"If you didn't do it, who did?" I asked.

"Search me," he said shrugging his shoulders. "Come on. I'll show you guys my house. I've got a few ice cold Molsons in the fridge."

"I don't know," I said reluctantly.

"We'll come. It's early, On, and remember how you said you wanted to show me a nice time while I was up here so that I wouldn't be a stranger?"

I grumbled. "Oh, okay," I grumbled. "But, we should at least go back and get the car before it gets dark."

Marti and I retraced our steps through the woods, got the car and drove down out of the condo entrance and up the first drive farther east. The sun now hung lower in the sky. "You didn't tell me there were such hot guys up here, On."

"Hot? As in fire-starter-hot?"

"Don't think so."

"Oh? And why is that?"

"He's too cute. He's good looking enough to be gay but those aren't the looks of an arsonist or a murderer."

"Yeah, right."

"He's a friend of yours, isn't he?"

"Not really. I just know him because we both grew up around here. He graduated a couple of years behind me."

"You're saying he could still be a suspect," she said restating the obvious.

"Duh."

"Oh, duh, shmuh," she said in a spiteful parody of the clever comment I'd uttered earlier.

"I'm just saying, be careful. He could be involved."

"Okay, mom," she said as we finished our climb up the gravel drive. Off to our right was a grove of apple trees. There was only a patch of grass in the yard but everything looked orderly. Frank came out on his porch and leaned on the railing, watching as we walked up a stepping stone path to the house. "This place is so cute!" squealed Marti, still in kittenish mode.

I grimaced, but Frank grinned, "Thanks. I'll give you a quick tour and then we can kick back on the deck here and watch the sunset.

Hot Property

The house was a log cabin with a porch across the entire front. As Frank said, it was small, but well laid out. We entered directly into his living room. He saw me gazing at the multi-colored stone wall behind his wood stove.

"I love rocks and most of these stones came from this property," he said.

"Did you build this place yourself?" I asked.

"Every inch of it. For some things, like that wall, the plumbing and electrical, I had a lot of help from friends."

We continued through the house. The kitchen behind the living room was compact and neat. He pulled three Molson beers from the refrigerator and handed us each one. We continued on to the two bedrooms and bath on the first floor then up to the loft bedroom and bath. "On stormy nights I can lie in my bed up here and watch the thunderclouds and lightning sweep across the valley."

"That sounds so romantic," Marti cooed, much to my disgust.

We traipsed back downstairs and out to the front porch and sat on a long glider. The expansive view down the hill and across the valley was dazzling. To the east, that is. To the west, it had probably once been even more beautiful. That is until a certain condominium project had marred the landscape.

"Now I see why you were so against the condos," I said. "They're a real eyesore from here."

"Sure are. I never would have built here if I'd known that they'd allow something like that. I thought I was safe. This was all zoned farm/forest." He took a swig of beer and continued, "Oh, I knew someone could build there but I thought it would be one house, like the zoning allowed. Not a whole frigging development."

"It's not right. People should be able to rely on zoning restrictions. Why did the planners allow that to happen?" Marti asked.

"They tried to stop it but they got scared off. The developers filed lawsuits against the township. Their attorney warned them that it could bankrupt the township if they lost. So they caved." He took another swig of his beer and then set the bottle on the porch floor, beside him. "Anyway, other than myself, who do you think might have done it, Onalee? I mean the murder."

"Geesh, I don't know." I looked at my watch. "What I do know is that we'd better be heading back to P-Town. I've got to work tomorrow." I stood up. Thanks for the brew. And the tour." As I set my half-finished beer on the deck railing, Marti shot me a less then friendly look.

Frank, not seeing it, smiled and said, "Hey it was cool running into you guys. And great meeting you, Miss Marti."

That brought out her dimples again. "I'll be here for a few days. Maybe we'll run into you again, Frank."

"I hope so." He said as he walked us to the car.

As we wound down beneath the trees along the driveway, Marti lit into me, "Since when do you go to bed at 9:00? I didn't even have time to finish my beer."

"Marti, the guy is a suspect in both an arson case and a murder investigation. Take your pick. I didn't feel at liberty to discuss the case with him. And, I don't think you should be going around, batting your eyelashes at him either. At least not until, if and when, he's cleared."

"Lighten up, Onalee."

Ignoring her childish outburst, I continued reasonably, "Besides, I do need to get a lot of work done tomorrow." I guess she heard me but my remarks dropped like stones into the pond of silence that had enveloped the car.

Back at my house we pulled out an airbed for Marti. My house has two bedrooms, one of which is the nerve center for O'Conner Appraisals, Inc. Marti would have the entire living room as her bedroom.

As the airbed plumped up, I thought about an article I'd read recently about the best inventions of the past fifty years. Personal computers had made the list. But I wish they'd asked the man, or woman on the street. In fact, if I'd been asked, these $39.00 spare beds attached to their own pumps would have been very near the top of the list, though not as high as roller blades or microwave ovens.

I didn't share this insight with Marti since she still seemed to be a bit miffed at me. We took turns in my one bathroom and went to bed.

Chapter Nine

I tiptoed past Marti to go for my run. She didn't seem to hear me. It was cool outside, but had the feel of a warm day in the making. It seemed as though our freakishly hot, dry weather would continue for a while longer.

I wondered what Marti would do today while I worked. I had to inspect another industrial building, this one was in Charlevoix, about seventeen miles southwest of Petoskey. My inspection was at 1:00 and I planned to do some preliminary work on it this morning. Of course Marti might have other ideas. And, it turned out she did.

By the time I got back, forty minutes later, Marti was awake. After I showered, we decided to go back to our favorite pancake restaurant. Since it was a weekday morning and still early summer, we got a table right away.

"You know how people say you shouldn't drink any alcohol before, say, 5:00 at night?" she asked.

"Uh huh. Except, I've always felt that it's okay to have a beer with lunch when you're skiing," I said, not really knowing where she was going with this.

"Do you know if there's any rule like that about ice cream? I mean, I know it's not quite 8:30 in the morning. But, those ice cream filled crepes smothered with raspberries are calling to me."

"Aha," I said eyeing her with new appreciation. The waitress came then and Marti sallied forth into gluttony as she ordered her ice cream crepes with coffee. "Make that a double," I said. As I always sometimes say, if you're going to go to a restaurant with great food, it's best to go with someone with a deep streak of decadence.

After our fabulous breakfast (or should we call it dreakfast, or, bressert?) I went off appraising and Marti started her day by going downtown and doing what she called her "cutesy shopping" before heading to the beach. We planned to meet up at about 5:00 at the Green Door for dinner.

*****

I was fairly productive and everything went well in Charlevoix. The property I was appraising was a steel fabricating building. Inside the shop area it had overhead cranes, like giant hooks, that are used to hoist heavy materials and move them around the building.

Hot Property

My eyes rose up to its distant ceiling heights.

"How much clearance do you have?" I asked Ron, the owner.

"Thirty-four feet under the hooks. The ceiling is forty feet." We heard a beeping noise and had to scurry out of the way as a forklift shot by. Maybe it was the sugar talking but it had been a dream of mine for a long time, so I popped up with, "I'd sure like to drive one of those things sometime."

Ron gave me an odd look, then said, as if he hadn't heard me, "Yes, well, come on and I'll show you the tool room." It seemed that that, as they say, was the end of that. Resigned, I snapped a few more photos and followed Ron. Another perk of this job is that you get to go into men's restrooms.

How many women can say they've been in thousands of men's restrooms all up and down the great state of Michigan? I glanced around. Hmmm, come to think of it, maybe it isn't such great grounds for bragging rights.

We finished the tour, shook hands and I promised to call him with the questions that come up as the appraisal process continues.

★★★★★

Later, over dinner Marti excitedly told me about her fabulous finds in Petoskey's famed (at least according to the Chamber of Commerce brochures) Gas Light District. Apparently she'd been able to lop off a large chunk of her Christmas shopping, not to mention the fact that she'd gotten a good start on her tan.

We both said no to desert. Marti felt as I did that if the day starts off with ice cream crepes, a line should be drawn at having two sugar fests in one twenty-four hour time span. We ordered a couple of decaf coffees and let it go at that.

"I spent quite a bit of time thinking about the case at the beach, today, and here's what I think we should do," Marti informed me as we sipped our coffees.

"Forget about it and let the police solve it?"

"Yeah, right," she laughed. "We need to make a list of all of the possible suspects and then figure out how we can interview each one of them."

"When are you going back?"

"When I get good and ready to, and that will be after we've made some headway on this case. Besides Frank is taking me to lunch tomorrow." With that she flounced out of her chair, leaving me at the table. Sputtering the whole way, I got to my feet and followed in her wake.

Chapter Ten

Back at the house, Marti dug a yellow legal pad and pencil out of her briefcase and perched on my couch. I sat on the other end of it. "Let's draw up our list of suspects. Who's number one?"

"Frank, the arsonist."

Marti scowled, "Get serious. He's not an arsonist and he's certainly no murderer."

"Marti. You barely know him. And, you don't know that he isn't. Put him on the list."

"Okay, I'll put him down, but not in the top spot, because he didn't do it." I watched her write his name on about line 15 on the page.

"Are you double-spacing? Because there aren't that many suspects."

"Start naming them, missy," she snapped.

"Okay, there's Mike Lorian," I said.

"He's the partner, right?"

"Yeah. And there's possibly Linda Lorian, Mike's wife who was having an affair with Jonathon."

"Whoa. Johnathon was sleeping with his partner's wife?"

"Yup. What are you smiling about?"

"That knocks Frank even further down the list."

"That's one interpretation of the data, I suppose. There's also Janet Richmond."

"The vic's wife?"

"Yes."

"Who else?"

"Well Marissa, in Jonathon's office mentioned that she thought the list should also include a township official or two, since they almost lost their jobs over the zoning mess; and maybe some old or current loves. She specifically mentioned the secretary."

"Okay." She wrote those down, each on their own line.

"And you, of course."

"Hey, come on, you know I didn't do it."

"Do I? And even if I may have my doubts, you are still a suspect," she said beginning to write my name.

"At least put me below your arsonist."

74

She sighed, "All right. He may have had more motive." She blotted me out of line seven and then penciled me in below Frank.

"Thanks."

"Any others?"

"Don't think so," I said.

"Okay, then. Let's go back through them one by one and figure out a way we can talk to each of them. First, Michael Lorian?"

"Done. Yesterday, when I re-inspected the condos."

"Okay, and did he say anything significant?"

"Twice he said that it will turn out to be the 'Tree-hugger/arsonist'." I looked over at her pad. "You're not writing that down."

"No. I'm not going to write down dumb comments. Just the ones that make sense and that will further our case."

"If you're not going to do this right, then let me do it," I said making a grab for the legal pad.

She pulled it away. "All right," she said. After she wrote that down she asked, "Now what about Janet Richmond? Do you know her?"

"Nope. But my friend Rhonda does. She's mentioned that their dogs play together sometimes." We went through the rest of the group and found that it was only Linda Lorian who was going to be hard to get to talk to. We could always drop in on township people and also Secretary Susie. As for "other loves and jealous husbands", we didn't even have names attached to any at this point.

"Okay, it's time to call, um, Rhonda," Marti said reading from her list.

I glanced at my watch. "It's only 9:15. That's not too late to call her." I punched in the numbers on the phone.

"Hello there, Onalee," she said after she picked up.

"Hi, Rhonda. You've got caller ID, eh? I was wondering if my friend Marti and I could walk with you and Gi Gi tomorrow? . . . Great, see you then. Bye."

I turned to Marti, "Tomorrow morning at 7:30."

"7:30?" She yelped.

"I'll make sure you're up."

"Thanks," she said sounding insincere.

I glanced outside. "Come on Marti," Want to go for a walk? We can catch a sunset while we're at it."

We walked along the beach at the county park. Towards 10:00, we saw a number of people knotted on the various wooden decks that jut out from the campground overlooking the beach and the lake. The sun was low in the sky now and its descent became more rapid as it started to flatten out a bit on top. "Maybe tonight's the night."

"You're still on the flash quest?"

"Yes. Why not us? We're good people. Many, many others have seen the green flash. I think it's our turn."

As we watched, the sun slid down, down and then below the horizon. Scarlets, oranges and purples arced across the sky as low hanging clouds glowed within from the sun's reflection. Another spectacular sunset. But, I'd have to wait for another night for a sight of the much touted but rarely observed green flash.

*****

The following morning, after a run and a struggle to awaken Marti, we set off for the nature trail. Rhonda and Gi Gi were already there. Rhonda looked pointedly at her watch. "I knew when I said 7:30, I wouldn't see you until at least 7:45 so I aimed for that and I still had to wait."

"Sorry. It's mostly my fault," Marti said with a yawn. She extended her hand, "Hi, I'm Marti Gonzalez."

"Hi. I'm Rhonda," she said, shaking Marti's hand. "And I just want to go on record as saying that I hate this so-called 'appraiser time' thing. You ought to try my job as a lawyer, and see what a judge would think of it." She turned and opened up the rear door of her car. A big, wooly dog leaped out and ran up to me.

"Gi Gi. Hello." I sat on my haunches and hugged her.

"Wow, what kind of dog is she?" Marti asked.

"Standard poodle."

"She's gorgeous, but she doesn't have the frou-frou hair cut like most of them."

"No. I don't like them. But if she ever makes me mad enough I keep telling her that instead of grounding her, I'll make her get groomed just like those show dogs on TV. I'll even put a pink bow in her hair and have them put those cute little balls of fur on top of her butt. She'll be a laughing stock to all of her doggie friends."

"Oh Gi Gi. Your mom is so mean to you," I said, lapsing into baby talk as I fondled her ears and looked into her beautiful almond shaped dark eyes. I got to my feet and we started meandering down the path through the hardwood forest.

"Has Gi Gi ever had puppies?" Marti asked.

"Not yet."

"Have you thought about mating her with a lab? You know those labradoodles are all the rage now," Marti said.

"Yes I know. They're breeding all kinds of dogs with poodles to try to get dogs that don't shed. A popular one right now is the schnauser poodle mix called shnoodles.

"But you're not into that kind of thing, are you?" I asked.

"No. But I have thought of starting a new mix. Crossing her with a wolf."

"Oh yeah? They'd be beautiful," I said.

"Yes, and you could call the puppies woodles. Or, if you'd rather, poofs."

"Oh geesh." Marti exclaimed.

We were coming into a meadow. "So what brings you two out at 8:00 on a Wednesday morning?" Rhonda turned towards us and asked.

"Did you read in the paper about the murder of Jonathon Richmond, the developer of Whispering Pines?"

"Yes," she said, frowning slightly.

"I remembered you saying that you sometimes walk Gi Gi with Janet Richmond and her dog."

"Yes, I do. Quite a bit, as a matter of fact. But, what does that have to do with you?"

"Actually, I was the one who found his body."

She stopped. "Really. Wow."

"Since I kind of got involved, I'd just like to talk to her. But I don't know her."

We were all walking down the path again. "Are you two playing Trixie Beldon?"

"Something like that I guess," I said.

"I thought you were reading too many detective novels, Onalee. Now I know for sure."

"So you'll help us?" Marti chimed in.

"I didn't say that. I don't know." She stopped again and turned towards me. "She just lost her husband. This isn't a game, you know."

"I do know. I'm a suspect, too, since I found the body." I paused. "But, if you're uncomfortable with it that's okay. Just forget it."

Marti again piped up, "But of course you realize that the police are always swamped and don't have much time to actually solve cases. All we're trying to do is bring to justice the cold-blooded creature who performed this despicable act."

Rhonda looked from Marti to me, "Look, if I introduce you guys, you've got to promise me you'll be really careful about what you say to her, okay?"

"We will. I promise," I said.

"Okay, I'll see what I can do."

* * * * *

I spent the day working on the Charlevoix industrial building. Meanwhile, Marti played tourist again and, borrowing my bike, went for a long ride around the bay in the morning. She had great weather for it, sunny and warm but not hot. It was also unusually still, with no wind off the lake to battle against. She got back about 11:50, showered and drove over to the Green Door to meet Frank at about 12:15. Only fifteen minutes late, I noted. She must really be smitten to go to all of that effort. Meanwhile I had, as I said, a very productive day.

That is, until the UPS truck dropped off a large package with my name on it. The return address listed "Splendors by Suzanne". That could only mean one thing. After carefully opening the box, I dipped my hands inside and pulled out . . . an opaque green plastic bag. I cut open the bag and out spilled the chiffoniest, cloyingly sweetest pile of pink ruffles I'd ever seen in one place. Even the ruffles had ruffles. Shouldn't there be some kind of law governing the number of flounces per garment? Maybe it was time for me to put aside my natural tendency towards political apathy and run for public office if this was what our country was coming to.

"Call me right away, when you get the dress." Rosie's excited voice flashed across my mind. I needed to gather my gumption and try it on. Maybe it will look better on than off, I told myself. I changed into it and got it completely smoothed out with all of the parts in the right places before I turned to the full length mirror.

Okay, I had the answer to one question. It had actually been better off than on. Ahhhhghghgh. Was this a cruel hoax? And yet, I needed to call Rosie.

Rosie was ecstatic that the dress came and fit. I told her the color was fine. I do, normally, love pink. We didn't get into the flounce count. After all, I'd kind of expected something like this right from the beginning. Rosie is unorthodox in many ways and it was her wedding. Her big day. If she wanted acres of pink ruffles, then pink ruffles it would be.

*****

Around 4:00, Marti wandered in. She stuck her head in my office to say hi and then stepped into the bathroom. "Whoa. That's a lot of pink." She bee-lined back to my office. "That's not a present for me is it?"

"Don't worry. It's all mine. Didn't I tell you I was going to be a bridesmaid for my friend Rosie?"

"Yes. But, you said she was a good friend, didn't you?"

"The best. Just like you only a bit more unconventional."

"I'll say, but you'll look lovely, Onalee. Pink is one of your best colors. When is this shindig? I might be able to come," she said a grin spreading over her face."

"It's close friends and family only. You keep yourself far away from me and my pink frock."

*****

I worked on the report for a bit longer and logged off the computer. Marti was sprawled in a lounger on my deck. "So how did your big date with Frankie the Felon go?" I asked.

She looked up. "I had a great time, despite what you might think." Her voice tinged with frost.

"Did you grill him? What did you find out? I certainly hope you didn't just sit around engaging in outrageous flirtation, when you could have been performing solid detective work." My fists were astride my hips as I badgered her.

"We did discuss the case, but as he told us at his house the other night, he didn't even know anything had happened until he heard the sirens."

I looked at my watch. "You've been gone for almost four hours. The service is always fast at the Green Door so what have you been doing all of the rest of the time?" I said, relentless in my interrogation.

"Ah, it was a fun date." She smiled, "We had a long leisurely lunch with a couple of beers, each. Then we went to the beach and just walked and talked. We have so much in common."

"You always did like bonfires as I recall."

★ ★ ★ ★ ★

That evening Marti filled me in on more details of her afternoon and watched while I chopped carrots, cauliflower and garlic, marinated a chunk of tofu and then put together a large wok of stir fry. Meanwhile a pot of brown rice simmered on another burner.

As we were finishing our dinner the phone rang. It was Rhonda. The girl works fast. We were to pick up Gi Gi tomorrow morning and then meet Janet Richmond and her dog at the nature trail. "Just tell her I have to be in Traverse City at 8:00 in the morning for depositions so I got you to watch Gi Gi for the day. It's true, too, so you guys will have to walk her again about 3:00. Is that okay?"

"Sure. And thanks."

"Just remember what I told you. Be gentle with her. And, Onalee, don't be late. Janet's always on time. Let's see, she has shoulder length brown hair and she's about average height. Her dog is a golden retriever named Lucas. He'll know Gi Gi and will come running over to you guys. Happy sleuthing."

Chapter Eleven

The following morning, Marti, Gi Gi and I scrambled to arrive at the nature trail on time. The parking lot was empty except for one other car. As I was letting Gi Gi out, another dog bounded up the small hill from the trail. Gi Gi was straining at her leash trying to get to him. She was stronger than I'd remembered and she dragged me with her. The other dog was a reddish golden retriever. I unhooked Gi Gi's leash and the two dogs tore off together.

A woman approached us, smiling and holding a leash. I recognized her from the funeral. She was the person with the page boy hair cut who had been sitting next to Mike Lorian, crying.

"Are you with Gi Gi?"

"Yes. We're walking her for Rhonda. She said we'd meet up with another dog she knows," I said.

"The two of them are best friends. Where's Rhonda?" She asked, as she continued to walk towards us.

"In Traverse City taking depositions," I said.

"Oh. Hi, I'm Janet," she said extending her hand, "And that wild puppy over there is Lucas."

"Hello. I'm Onalee O'Conner," I said shaking her hand.

"And I'm Marti Gonzalez."

Janet was staring at me, "Onalee. That's such an unusual name. You're not . . . the one . . . the one who. . ." she frowned.

"Who found your husband's body?" I said quietly. "Yes, it was me."

"And you're a friend of Rhonda's?" She asked, clearly puzzled.

"Yes, Rhonda and I have known each other for years. We grew up in the same neighborhood on Jennings Street."

"Oh. Rhonda's never mentioned you."

"We don't see each other all that often, these days, but we keep in touch. I'm really sorry for your loss. I didn't know your husband well, but he was always nice to me."

She gave me a hard look, "No doubt."

"Oh no. It wasn't like that." I said, feeling my cheeks redden as I rushed to reassure her. "I'm an appraiser and I valued some of his properties. At other times I had called him to get information and he always helped me out."

She looked away and brushed her cheek. "Yes. That sounds like him. In a lot of ways, he was a great guy." She looked around, "Lucas. Lucas. Where did those dogs go?"

Oh no. I'd already forgotten my responsibility. Where was Gi Gi? We trotted down the trail into the woods, calling to the dogs as we went.

"There they are," said Marti, pointing towards the woods at our left. "They're getting a drink of water from the creek."

We slowed to a walk. "Do those dogs ever quit playing?" I asked hoping to put Janet at ease again.

She smiled a little, "Oh, eventually they'll get tired. They sure do get a kick out of being together." We hiked along in silence for a while.

"Lucas is such a beautiful dog. Do you plan on breeding him?" Marti asked, breaking the silence.

"No, he's been neutered."

"Did your husband ever take him hunting?" Marti asked.

"I suppose you could say that." She paused. "There was at least a time or two that Jonathon walked Lucas down at the waterfront, hoping to hunt down new girlfriends." Her attempt at a smile looked more like a grimace.

Again a silence fell over the three of us, as we tromped through the trees. Then I ventured, "Janet, do you think . . . would one of his girlfriends go to the extent of killing him?"

Her face clouded over. Gees, I'd probably gone too far.

Surprisingly, she answered, "He had his women, there's no denying that. In fact, there was a constant stream of them. But you know what?" She stopped and turned back towards us. "In the end, he always got tired of them and came back to me. So, yes, any of those bimbos might have thought she was in love with him and then killed him . . . after he broke her heart," she said sourly.

"Anyone in particular you can think of?" Marti asked, getting right to the point.

"I would think it would probably be one of his more recent affairs. The women from previous years have probably gone on to other conquests by now." Janet shook her head slightly, her mouth pulled into a grim line.

"Do you know who he was seeing lately?" Marti forged on with her line of questioning.

Janet shook her head. "Usually all I know is the rumors I hear."

"What was the word on the street?" I asked.

"Three words, actually. Linda Pendleton-Lorian."

"His partner Mike's wife?" I asked, trying to sound like I hadn't heard it before. We'd all stopped again and Janet stood facing Marti and I.

"Oh, yes," she said and then turned and plowed on through the forest. We trotted to catch up to her.

"Wow. Did Mike know?" Marti called out to her stiffened back.

She slowed a bit and said over her shoulder, "If not, then he is the only person north of Toledo who didn't."

"Could she have killed him?" The relentless Marti asked.

Slow down Girl or Janet may shut us right out. I cleared my throat, "If you ask me, anyone who hyphenates her name is capable of anything."

"Yeah, I don't like those name hyphenators either," Marti chimed in.

Janet was smiling again.

"But seriously," I said, hoping we could get things back on track, "Do you think Linda Lorian did it? Or, maybe Mike Lorian killed

90

Jonathon when he found out his wife was two timing him with his partner."

Janet stopped again and turned towards us, "I honestly don't know. Linda is a volatile person. And I heard that she fell for him pretty hard." She thought a moment. "Now, Mike? I wouldn't think so. He doesn't strike me as the type that would kill anyone. He's always seemed like a really nice guy who's unfortunately married to a real bitch." She looked thoughtful again, gazing into the nearby stand of birch trees. "Then again, maybe he's one of those guys who isn't so nice when you really get to know him."

"Any others?" Marti pressed. "We heard he always had a couple on the string."

"Well, my guess is that Amber would be the other current fling," Janet said as she turned and again started walking down the path.

"Amber?" I asked as Marti and I trailed after her. "Who is Amber?"

"The receptionist at R & L," Janet said, without breaking her stride.

Ah, A.K.A. Susie Secretary.

"I heard they might have been involved." Marti paused and then asked in a soft voice, "How were you with all of this?"

That brought her to a halt again. She looked directly at us. "Neither of you is married are you?"

"No," we both said.

"I can tell. It's different when you are. You put up with more than you ever dreamed you could. You don't want to rock the boat.

"Oh sure, we fought about it, especially the first few times it happened. And, I cried and begged him to tell me why I wasn't enough for him, but," she paused. "In the end I always waited around until each one ran its course and he came back to me. I used to think of him as my homing pigeon. He always came back." Again she laughed but her eyes looked sad.

"You know, I played a little game sometimes. I'd bet myself how long they'd last. I got pretty good at it. Linda Lorian? Correction: Linda Pendleton-Lorian." She stepped a couple of feet off the trail and pulled a bag out of her pocket. Reaching down, she scooped up after her dog.

"Anyway," she continued, while knotting the plastic bag, "I had to be honest with myself. I figured with her beauty and ability to charm the socks off any male, she'd last a good three months. Not to mention the added thrill of her being Jon's partner's wife. That might actually buy her another month." She sighed.

92

"Well, I guess it might have, if he hadn't gotten killed."

"He was involved with both Linda P-Lorian and Amber during the last few weeks?" Marti asked.

"As far as I know, yes."

"Do you think the two of them knew about each other?" I asked.

"I guess you'd have to ask them," she said.

Following Lucas and Gi Gi, we continued on down the trail. Then I said, "There are other people on the list of suspects too, I think, like some of the township officials and Frank Ryan the guy who lives by Whispering Pines. Actually, you and I are also on that list."

"Is that why you're doing this?" Janet looked at me, searchingly. "Because you're a suspect?"

"Partly and also because I feel like I got involved when I found his body."

"Well, all I can tell you is, that my life was a whole lot better with Jonathon than without him, so you're wasting your time if you think I did it."

"No, we don't think you did it. And we're also quite positive that Frank Ryan is innocent." Marti added.

Janet's head swiveled towards Marti, "That whacko arsonist? What makes you think he's innocent?" she asked.

"We know him and he isn't capable of something like that, or of arson." Marti said, standing by her man.

"Janet," I said in a gentle tone, "do you mind if I ask where you were when Jonathon was killed?"

She turned away and when she faced us again, her eyes were brimming with tears. "I was probably right here when it happened. Walking Lucas. I'd had a busy morning that day so I put off his long walk until the afternoon." She paused, "We . . . we got home and I was," she wiped a hand across her eyes and sniffed.

"Sorry. I used to rely on Jon for tissues. He was always good for one, and even if it was slightly used, we shared it." She looked at us with a teary smile. "Anyway, I was starting to fix dinner when the police came. In other words, I was alone the whole time. In one fell swoop, I lost my husband and became the prime suspect in his murder. You know they always look to the spouse first.

"In this case, Detective Costas assumes I have a strong motive since everyone in town knows Jon cheated on me." She turned to me, her face hardening with resolve. "So, if you're really going to try to solve this thing, and you're not just playing at it, I'll do anything I can to help you."

By now we had nearly circled back to the beginning of the trail. Lucas and Gi Gi were trotting along side by side several feet off the path. I seized the opportunity. "Do you know how we can get an interview with Linda Pendleton-Lorian?"

She called Lucas to her and leaned over to snap his leash on. "Let's see. Her daughter is always playing tennis at the Racket Club and I've heard that Linda P. goes to watch quite often. You could casually meet up with her there, I would think."

"Do you know when they're usually there?" I asked, as I put Gi Gi on her leash.

"My guess is that mornings would be good. I probably could find out for you."

"That would be great. Here's one of my O'Conner Appraisal Company cards with my phone number on it. Janet, thank you so much for talking with us."

Chapter Twelve

"Wow, that was a lucky break," Marti said as we drove back to the house. "I was afraid she would tell us to go fly a kite."

"I know. But I'm sure she wants this case solved as much as anybody." I put the blinkers on and we rounded a corner by the high school. "What are you up to today?"

"I'm meeting Frank for lunch again, but he's got to work so I think I'll mosey on over to the beach after that. What about you?"

"Working, though I might stop over to the township hall and nose around a bit."

She turned to me, grinning. "Ooh. That sounds like more fun than the beach. I'll come too."

"Actually, I kind of wanted to go by myself. I've known them all for a long time and I think they might talk more, one on one."

"I suppose you're right," she sighed.

"Hey, don't worry, I'll fill you in on everything."

Hot Property

*****

After changing into lightweight slacks and a beige short-sleeved sweater, I spent the morning driving by comparable industrial buildings. At one point I was near the township offices and stopped in to try to catch the supervisor, Roger Bandsinger. From what I'd heard, he'd taken the most heat from Jonathon Richmond, but he wasn't in.

As it happened he was also the one at the township that I knew the best. I left a message for him to call me when he could, then returned to the road to drive by more comparable properties. At about noon, I picked up a couple of protein bars. Then I stopped in a shady spot on the shore of Crooked Lake.

As I ate my lunch I watched a group of kids splashing around in the blue-green shallows. Although it was mid-June, Crooked Lake is a small lake, for these parts, and it is often warm enough to swim in by this time, at least by a child's standards.

As I munched, I slipped into reflection. These kids are lucky I thought. September is far away and a whole summer of possibilities stretches out in front of them. This is the time of year when I miss being ten-yearsold. Growing up in northern Michigan for me meant taking a free bus to the beach every morning and spending every afternoon in the backyard playing with the neighborhood kids. Whiffleball, croquet and kick the can were games we never got tired of.

After finishing the last tasty morsel of my peanut butter bars, I cruised by more industrial buildings, stopping to take a few notes and pictures. By about 2:30, I was finished and found myself no more than a couple miles from the R & L office. Twas a perfect time to drop in for a wee chat with Amber, AKA Susie Secretary.

There were no cars in the parking lot when I arrived at R & L, and no one was in the front office area except Susie, I mean Amber. Darn Marissa, that Susie Secretary thing was annoyingly stuck in my brain. She was talking on the phone as I entered the building. Finally, she looked up and a small frown creased her forehead, as she appeared to be trying to place me. It seemed to be a personal call and she ended it abruptly.

"Hi. I'm Onalee O'Conner, the appraiser for Whispering Pines."

"Oh, yeah, hi. What can I do for you?" She said barely containing her lack of excitement.

"I had some more questions. Is Mike Lorian here today?" I asked, hoping that since his car wasn't here, he wouldn't be either.

"No, you just missed him." She said studying her nails.

"Shoot." I gave her a little conspiratorial smile.

"I'll bet on such a gorgeous day he's playing hooky on the golf course."

She wasn't buying into it. "Actually, I believe he is meeting with clients to discuss details of their proposed project," she said, stiffly, and then turned towards her computer monitor.

"Oh, so he's going to continue ahead with R & L on his own," I said, hoping I wasn't being summarily dismissed.

She leveled a stony gaze at me, "So it would seem."

Nothing was getting through to this Queen of Cool. I leaned in closer over her desk, "I've got to tell you, that's the first time I've ever found a dead body on an inspection. It sure can shake you up." It was a last ditch effort at determining if intelligent life existed within that body mass.

She swiveled around from her computer and stared at me. "I didn't know it was you who found Jonathon. How terrible."

"It was a shock. I'd known him for a long time and he seemed like a sweet guy."

"He was. The best boss ever."

"I hope he didn't try to hit on you. I heard the gossip."

99

She looked away. "What did you hear?" she asked in a small voice.

"That he had been spending time with Linda P.-Lorian. Was that true?"

"I think I heard something like that." She said, now looking down at her keyboard.

"Wow. I hope Mike Lorian never found out."

"Why?" She asked, turning towards me.

"Well, because, it might cause real trouble in their marriage."

She leveled her eyes at me. "Yeah, like they were the Brady bunch or something. If she was running around on him, wouldn't you say it was already a bit too late for their marriage?"

Spoken from the vantage point of the other woman. "Probably," I said, assuming I might get farther by agreeing with her. "What's she like?"

"Linda?"

"Yes."

"She's one of those women who thinks she's better than any other woman in the room." Her voice was heated. "And at the same time she's on the make for every guy around her," she said, then resumed staring at her screen. "I think she's disgusting." She paused. "But, of course, she's a real hit with the men."

"Does she come in here very much?"

"More often than we'd like."

"Was there anyone else that Jonathon was seeing besides her?"

She looked up again and her eyes narrowed, "Why are you asking all of these questions?"

"Because I'd like to know who killed Jonathon. I really liked him."

She again turned back to her computer and this time she started typing, her long nails clacking away. "Yeah, me too. I'll tell Mike you were looking for him."

I plunged ahead. "So, it was true about you and Jonathon."

Her nails froze in mid-air and this time when she looked up at me, her dark eyes glinted with fury. "Get out of here," she hissed.

Just then, the door opened and Marissa Martin entered into the charged atmosphere. She looked at Amber, then at me. "Hi. What's going on?"

"Hi Marissa. Nothing. Amber and I were just gossiping and I was on my way out." I brushed past her and strode through the door. Palms sweaty, I slid into my car seat. I turned the key, put the car into drive, and looked up to see that my exit was blocked by a dark grey sedan. Gnats.

Chapter Thirteen

It was the Costas-mobile.

"Ms. O'Conner. Lovely to see you. What brings you to the fortress of R & L Enterprises on this fine day?" His grin had a feral edge to it.

Why did I always blush around him? "I happen to be an appraiser by profession," I said haughtily. At least, I was striving for haughty.

"Yes, I remember. Find any more bodies on any of your inspections?"

"No, as a matter of fact I haven't."

"Good. Now if you'll just stick to the appraisal profession and leave the police work to us, then maybe we, and by that, I mean the other police officers and myself; can push forward and solve this case. Do you get my drift?"

"Yes. I believe I do, Detective." Again I aimed for haughty but I fear I may have fallen short.

About 3:00, Gi Gi and I went on our appointed rounds. Then I worked on my appraisal until Marti dragged in, obviously tired from her rough day of power lunching and sun worshipping. We decided to take advantage of the continued unseasonably warm weather and grill out. Marti showered and then ran to the grocery store for meat for her and a bottle of wine for us both while I started the grill and made a salad.

Forty-five minutes later we were seated in lounge chairs, sipping our wine and waiting for the coals to die down. I told Marti about my day as she made notes in her yellow pad. We now had interviewed four of the known suspects: Jon Richmond's partner, Mike Lorian; Frank Ryan, the tree hugger; Janet Richmond and Amber the secretary. We didn't have a last name for her yet, but that was probably okay at this point in the investigation.

I poured us each a second glass of wine and then put Marti's meat and my bean burger on the grill as far apart as possible. I thought Marti might be sufficiently loosened up now. "So how was your lunch with Frank?" I inquired, being careful to sound non-judgmental.

"Oh fine. We had a great time."

"Where did you go?"

"To that great restaurant on Howard Street that you've taken me to before. They have scrumptious lunches."

"Indeed they do. I love their sandwiches as well as their pies," I said, keeping my tone warm, chit chatting away before getting down to business. "So, did you find out anything more from him?" Using separate spatulas, I flipped both burgers then put two sets of buns on cooler areas of the grill.

She frowned. "No. He doesn't know anything else, as we've both tried to tell you. Repeatedly, I might add."

"Don't get upset. It can't hurt to ask." I said mildly as I carefully lifted each of the buns to check for doneness. Not quite yet. I turned back to Marti. "Just be sure he sticks to the same story."

She sighed. "Of course he'll 'stick to the same story', it's the truth."

"Did you talk about it at all?"

"As a matter of fact we did. He figures it was probably a jealous girlfriend or husband, given Richmond's reputation."

The buns were golden and the burgers were done. I scooped them both up and placed them on our plates. "Were there any other environmentalists who might have been enraged enough to do it?" I asked as I spooned green salsa on my burger.

"Frank doesn't think so. He says that there were plenty of people upset about the project but that unfortunately he is the one who is most directly affected. Well, other than the township zoning guys." She took a bite, then closed her eyes. "Mmmm, yum, this is a good burger, On. I love the blue cheese in the middle."

"Thanks. The O'Conner kitchens aim to please. We munched in silence for a few minutes. Now who could that be?" My cordless phone was ringing.

"Hello? Oh, hi! . . . Just finishing dinner. . . Not much, mostly just working. How about you?" We had been sitting on the deck and I walked down the steps to the backyard to distance myself from certain over curious ears.

We chatted a few more delicious minutes then I hung up and sauntered back up the stairs, trying not to grin.

Marti said, "So who was that?"

I smiled in spite of myself, "Rick Sommers."

"What? He calls you?" Her voice was shrill. "And, at this hour? It's way past 5:00 in the morning." Her eyes narrowed with suspicion then she chuckled, "You've got something going on with him don't you. Why'd you hold out on me?"

"Well, it's nothing really," I hedged.

"Yeah right," she said a big grin on her face. "He sure is a cutie. It's about time you quit moping around. You've been in mope-mode ever since your break-up with the Odious Tim."

"I was not moping."

"You were and it was unattractive, I might add." She got up and started dancing around me. "Onalee and Rickie sittin' in a tree, K-I-S-S-I-N-G."

* * * * *

About 11:00, as we were getting ready for bed, Marti said, "Know what, On? I've got to get back home and get some work done."

"When are you going?"

"Tomorrow morning."

The following day, Friday, Marti left as I set off for my run. She gave me instructions to call after each of my interviews and with any new breakthroughs on either "our case" or with the dashing Mr. Sommers.

The next couple of days were uneventful. As it turned out, it was a good thing that I had a bit of a breather before the events that lay ahead of me.

Chapter Fourteen

Monday morning, I finished jogging and walked the last block to cool off. A dry wind gusted by me and a cloud of dust eddied up. It was unsettling. When were we ever going to get rain? Where had our cool and rainy June days gone? This hot dry weather was just plain wrong for the north-country. The weatherman kept predicting rain, the woodland creatures, flowers and birds were crying out for it, but it just wouldn't come.

I opened my front door. The house seemed quiet without Marti's chatter. I worked on my appraisal for a while. By now, the file had grown thick with notes and leads and the report numbered sixty-three pages. About 10:30, Janet Richmond called to say that Linda Lorian's daughter was at tennis practice this morning. If I went right away, I could probably catch Linda P. So much for getting any more work done.

At a guess, the tennis club set was a bit ritzy so I decided to change out of my "work at home" attire, consisting of my old Toledo Open badminton shirt, and jeans into a pink and white striped polo shirt and pink capris. After that I jumped into my Honda and sped over to the Racket Club.

Inside the large steel and concrete building there were eight tennis courts with six of them in use. On two of them, there were women who appeared to be in their mid to late thirties, playing doubles. They were all trim and intent on their games. I don't think any of them even noticed me as I walked by. Two older men, also athletic looking, were on the next court. The next two each held two players, and they seemed to be volleying rather than in a game. Then I passed by two open courts before reaching one with a young girl obviously being coached.

She was tossing up ball after ball and hammering them just above the net. "That's great Sam, but let's see more spin," yelled her coach.

Sam was tall with long legs and wide shoulders. Her blond hair was pulled back into a ponytail. When did high schoolers become so glamorous? We had had a few pretty females in our class but now days it seems like the schools teem with gorgeous girls. The competition I'd faced had been stiff enough. The coach strode over to Sam and was showing her a better stroke as I meandered over to the courtside bleachers.

Hot Property

A woman who looked to be only slightly older than Sam sat absorbed in the action. For this informal event, she was wearing a sky blue silk shirt and khaki slacks. Several chunky gold bracelets encircled her tanned right wrist.

All the way over here, I had tried to think of a natural way to begin a conversation with this woman that I could then ease into a grilling session. I never had come up with anything. Winging it, I said, "She's quite a player."

Linda turned toward the sound of my voice, apparently noticing for the first time that another person occupied her bleacher. Her eyes glinted with the same beautiful blue as her shirt. A teensy bit too blue. Definitely the result of contact lens.

"Yes, she's a natural," Linda P. informed me and then turned back to the court.

I watched more blistering serves and then asked, "Does she play competitively?"

"Of course. She's the number one player at Petoskey High."

"Wow. Does she play singles or doubles?"

"Singles, obviously. The stronger players typically play singles."

"Oh. I guess I'm not really that well versed in tennis. I just like to hit the ball around." I smiled and extended my hand in the universal gesture of fellowship. "By the way, my name is Onalee O'Conner. I know your husband because I'm a real estate appraiser. He told me what a fabulous player your daughter was."

Ignoring my out-stretched hand, as well as my greeting, she said, "Mike does love to talk about his daughter," her eyes never leaving the court.

I seemed to be making no progress here. "Actually, Mike and I were talking when I was in his car coming back from inspecting Whispering Pines." That got her attention. "I wonder if we could talk about Jonathon Richmond a little."

"Who did you say you were?" She asked, turning around and appearing to actually see me for the first time.

"Onalee O'Conner."

"Do I know you?" She asked, a slight frown creasing her forehead.

"No. We've never met. I'm the one who found Jonathon Richmond's body at Whispering Pines."

"How terrible for you," she said, almost as if she meant it.

"Do you know who did it?"

"I have no idea. I'm not a policeman. Now, if you'll excuse me, I need to concentrate on

110

my daughter's tennis lesson." She turned away again.

"Where were you when Jonathon was killed?"

She snapped around again, eyes glaring, "Will you leave or shall I call security to throw you out?"

"I'll leave. Nice chatting with you, Ms. Lorian."

I descended the bleachers and walked across the floor, feeling her glare on my back the whole way. In reality, I'm sure I was flattering myself. More than likely, she was immediately reabsorbed into watching her daughter. Was she living vicariously through her? Did I care? No, except I would like to have been able to ask her some questions. Guess who now jumped to the top of my list of suspects? Miz P.-Lorian, of course. Anyone that nasty must be the murderer.

Chapter Fifteen

Since I'd already batted zero once today, I decided to see if I could strike out again. This time I'd go to the township and hunt up Roger Bandsinger.

The township offices were housed in a building that had been built for general offices. It was a one-story, long brick building that was about 25 years old. The original occupants had outgrown it at the same time that the township needed a new home and had purchased their facility.

Inside the front door there was an information desk and a receptionist. After a few moments of friendly backing and forthing, she told me that Roger was in and that she would call him to come to the lobby. Roger, a short, stocky man in his 50s, approached from my left.

"Hi Onalee." he said, smiling. "I'm sorry I didn't call you yesterday. I've been up to my eyeballs in work." He placed his hand on his forehead, illustrating the size of his to-do pile. "Anyway, what can I do for you?"

Hot Property

"Have you got a minute? I have a few questions for you."

"Sure. Come on back to my office." Roger led the way down the hall. The walls were painted silvery gray and the carpet was a darker gray. It was cool and institutional. Considering the heated zoning battles that were often pitched in this building, soothing colors were a smart idea. He stepped behind his desk and pulled out his chair. I sat in one of several chairs in front of it.

I decided to get right down to business. "Roger, what can you tell me about the problems out at Whispering Pines?"

His eyes narrowed. "You mean the zoning issues?"

"Yes. I know there were several lawsuits but I didn't keep up on the day-to-day stuff," I said.

"Well, as you probably know, all of that land out there was zoned Farm/Forest, and required two acres for each household. Then along comes R & L and they decide that our zoning is 'too restrictive' and that they should be allowed to plant a small city out there. Originally, they wanted twenty-two units per acre. Out there. In God's country, for Pete's sake. It was crazy.

"We told 'em we wouldn't allow it, so they came back with a plan for 20 units per acre.

Of course, we still wouldn't allow it, so they sued us." He shrugged his shoulders and then continued. "Our attorney told us that the cost to fight them in court would bankrupt the township. We held a public meeting to let people voice their opinions, and boy, did they ever. People came out of the woodwork to protest it. It wasn't just a few cock-eyed environmentalists, it was a lot of ordinary folks in the township who live up here for the quality of life."

"Wow. So what did you do?"

He shook his head, "It seemed like we had no choice. We gave them the go ahead for the development. But, we did, at least, get 'em down to eighteen units an acre." He looked me straight in the eyes. "Some victory, eh? They have a little over ten acres so Whispering Pines will eventually have 180 households."

"That's a huge development for around here. Did the people in the township back you up on it?"

"That depends on what you mean by 'backing us up.' I, as the supervisor, almost lost my job. They had a recall election. Fortunately, they didn't get quite enough votes to kick me out." He gave me a wry smile.

"But you were against the development."

"Yes, originally. But, then after I talked with our attorney and it looked like it was best to back down, I pushed for that. It was seen as caving in to the developers in some circles," he sighed. "It was a huge mess."

"How upsetting. And you were just trying to do what was right for the township."

"You've got it." His lips turned down as he shook his head. "This job used to be fun, but not anymore."

"It doesn't seem right that the developers should have that much power."

"Sure doesn't. But then unfortunately I don't get to make the rules."

"Do you think anything will change now that Jonathon Richmond is gone?"

"Gone?" He grinned, "You mean to that big condo project in the sky? Sorry."

I must have looked shocked at his light-hearted approach to Richmond's death.

"I hope you weren't close friends," he continued.

"No, but I did know him. He always treated me okay," I said.

"Oh, I'm sure he did. He either wanted you to give him a high appraised value or something else, let's just say, X-rated."

"Sounds like you think all of the rumors about his affairs were true."

115

Putting his right hand up, palm out, he said, "Hey, all I know is what I hear. I'd like to believe them just because I didn't like the guy and I wouldn't put anything past him. I guess I shouldn't tell you this stuff but it's off the record, okay?"

"Sure. Speaking on the q.t., then, who do you think killed him?"

"Search me."

"Can I ask, are you on the list of suspects?"

"I'm sure I was, at first. There was a pretty long list, you understand. But, I was out of town when it happened. In fact my wife and I were in downtown Thunder Bay, Ontario, at the exact time he was killed. I know because Detective Costas made me pinpoint my whereabouts. We'd decided to take a family vacation and go on the circle tour of Lake Superior. Gorgeous trip. You should do it sometime, Onalee."

"I plan to," I said. "Was there anybody else at the township who was also a suspect?"

He eyed me, "Now you're making me curious. Why all the questions about Richmond?"

"I was the one who found his body and I'm also a suspect."

"Oh, okay. Wow. I hadn't heard that. Did you do it?" His smile took the sting out of the question.

"No. I told you, I never had any problems with him. Anyway, do you think anybody else here might have done it?"

He became serious again. "I can't imagine it. I was the one who had gotten into the biggest mess because of him and like I say, I have an iron-clad alibi."

"What about some of the neighbors or environmentalists?"

"That's who I'd look to, if I were Costas. Well, or someone who was ticked off at all his skirt-chasing."

"Have you heard who he was spending time with lately?"

"Actually, running the township takes up a good bit of my time so I don't really spend all that much of my days gossiping." Then he leaned in a bit and lowered his voice, "Although, I do believe there was some scuttlebutt about his taking up with his partner's wife," He leaned back and shook his head. "What a scumbag."

"Yeah, I heard that too," I said nodding my head. "Anybody else?"

"I guess there was one right after the other but I really didn't keep a running score. Some of them seemed to be in his office, though, according to my sources."

"Roger, thanks. Would you do me a favor? If you hear anything else, would you call me?"

"Sure. Good luck, Onalee."

Back aboard the Honda, I drove toward my house. It was just about lunchtime. This detecting business sure builds up an appetite, I thought. All and all, I was making headway. I couldn't wait to fill Marti in on my latest interviews.

I wish she could have stayed longer, at least a few more days. And Frank, the tree-hugger was wishing the same thing, or I've missed my guess. Maybe it was a good thing she was gone. It might give that romance a chance to cool off a bit. She is a big girl and can date whom ever she chooses, but what if he is the murderer? Or even the arsonist? Marti never struck me as one of those women who would love having a penitentiary pen pal and live for conjugal visits.

Then again, maybe he is innocent, at least of these charges. His overall innocence I'd have to question. He always seemed to me to be one of those quiet types with a wide streak of wildness in him. On the other hand, Marti had grown up in Mexican Village in Southwest inner city Detroit and had put herself through college. She always seemed more than capable of handling anything that was thrown her way.

I pulled into my driveway with thoughts of yogurt and bran cereal swirling temptingly through my head. My heart was singing as I skipped up my front steps. I love that old expression that it's always darkest before the dawn, but in my experience there should be a corollary expression that goes something like, "The sky is the most brilliant before being blotted out by blackness." Or, something along those lines. I don't know, appraisers aren't known for their poetry. Anyway, I found my key without the usual fumbling search, opened the front door and screamed, "Oh my God."

Chapter Sixteen

Blood was everywhere. What had happened? Who
had been killed? I backed out the door and ran
over to my car. I jumped in and locked the
doors. Then I fumbled for my cell phone and
called 9-1-1. Finally, a man's voice answered.

"Hi, um, someone broke into my house. I-I
saw a lot of blood. I don't know what
happened, but I'm in my car now in my
driveway."

He asked for my name, address and phone
number and said the police were on their way.
I heard a light wrap on my car window and
looked up into the worried eyes of my
neighbor.

"Onalee. You look distraught. What's the
matter?"

I opened the window. "Hi, Mrs. Stirnaman.
Someone broke into my house. I just called the
police."

My neighbor had a shocked look on her face
as her hand fluttered to her mouth. "Onalee.
That's terrible. Why don't you come over to
the house with me? Julian and I are just

finishing our walk and I can fix you a nice cup of tea. And remember, you're to call me Maybelle."

Hearing his name, Julian, a regal looking golden retriever, looked up at me. I unlocked the car and climbed out.

Mrs. Stirnaman held out her arms, and I grabbed hold of her like a life buoy.

I had quit crying, but I was still shaking. The sound of sirens cut through the air. Soon, three police cars showed up and uniformed officers swarmed my property.

We stood watching as the patrolmen encircled my house. My home. My sanctuary. Where someone, in broad daylight, had entered and apparently killed someone. Or something.

Julian began tugging on the leash. He weighed almost as much as my neighbor.

"I'd better go and talk with the police," I told her.

"Would you like me to stay with you?"

I hope I'm that courageous and warm-hearted when I'm in my eighties. "No. But you've been great." I hugged her again then made my way towards my house. Glancing back, I saw her still standing by her handsome dog in a blue and white checked apron. "Thanks again," I called over to her.

Then, a too familiar, dark gray car sidled up to the curb and the window powered down.

"Is this your drama du jour Ms. O'Conner?"

Once again I found myself staring into the glacial blue eyes of Detective Costas. I turned away, not willing to dignify that remark with any reply.

"You know, if you'd just leave the detective work to the police, I think that you'd find life a lot easier. And safer."

"Thanks for the advice, Detective Costas," I said as I continued walking toward my house. Costas parked his car and stepped out to confer with some of the other policemen. I plodded to the back of my house then stopped and just stood there. Surveying the scene, my heart was nearly bumping up against my gizzard.

Glass was strewn all over the deck and my sheers, driven by the summery breeze, were billowing in and out of the hole where a window used to be. I shivered. What were the police finding in there? Whatever it was, human or animal, it had to be dead after losing so much blood.

I saw Costas, inside now, notice me through the window. He flipped the latch and stepped out through the patio door. "What did you find in there?" my voice sounded small and frightened. Clearing my throat, I willed myself to sound strong and confident in front of this too smug cop.

"Tell me what happened. From the beginning." He sat in one of my deck chairs and pulled another one directly across from him. "Relax. Have a seat."

"Thanks," I said, sitting down. I was relieved that my voice was more robust, even if my insides were still mush. "I came home for lunch, unlocked my front door and saw all of the blood. I ran back outside and called 9-1-1."

"So you didn't really go into your house."

"No. What did you find?" My voice was quivery again.

"Not much other than the red paint."

"Red paint? What about the blood and the body?"

"There is no blood, but if you just give it a passing glance, I suppose the paint could look like blood. There is also no body. There are, however, some chairs overturned and papers strewn around. But you'll have to tell us if anything is missing."

"By the way, I thought you usually work out of your house." He took a small pad of paper and a pen out of his breast pocket. "Where were you this morning?"

"Am I on trial here? I would prefer answers rather than questions about my whereabouts, Detective," I snapped.

He kept his voice even. "What I'm getting at is it seems risky for someone to break into your house if you're around most of the time. Did you tell anyone your schedule for the day?"

"Oh," I said. I shook my head. "No, but unless someone knew me pretty well, they might not know how much time I spend here." I looked at him. "You think it was the killer who broke in, don't you."

"All I know is, if I were a killer, and some Nancy Drew Wannabe started putting the heat on me, I wouldn't like it. And I might even have a go at her house, just to scare her a bit." He looked straight at me, eyes blazing in the sun, "This isn't a kid's game. You may find yourself in real hot water if you don't back off."

He stood up, "Walk through the house with me and see if you can tell if anything is missing."

Nothing seemed to be changed in the kitchen or dining room. The carpeting by the front door was still saturated in red and more red was smeared all over my couch. I stopped and stared at it and could see now that it was just paint. Who would do this to me?

A couple of chairs and my coffee table were overturned but unscathed. My bedroom and bathroom also were untouched. But my office was a shambles. For the second time that day, tears welled up in my eyes. I turned away for a moment to center myself. Then I forced myself to face the destruction.

Files had been taken out of my filing cabinet and dumped on the floor. It looked like someone had swiped an arm and knocked over my desk lamp and computer monitor. "I . . . I can't tell if anything is missing but . . . the big stuff, like my computer and TV are here. It looks like just damage was done."

"Do you have any reason to believe that the intruder might have been looking for something in your office?" he asked.

"No. I can't imagine what it would be. This is all," I had to swallow, "all appraisal stuff. It wouldn't really interest anyone."

"Okay, Ms. O'Conner," he said in a softer tone. "The first thing you're going to need to do is to call a glass place and get that window fixed. Have you ever considered installing an alarm system?"

"No, at least I never had." My voice was unsteady again. "I don't know now."

"You should consider it." We were walking back into the living room now. "Well, we're done here. But, call me if you find that

125

anything is missing, or if you do think of something that the intruder might have been looking for."

"Okay." I noticed that all of the other police had left the house. We walked outside, and I sank down on my front porch step.

He turned to me, "Are you going to be okay here, alone?"

My jaw dropped in spite of myself. Detective Costas, worried about me? I must look pretty pathetic. "This is nothing compared with missing a deadline on an appraisal. I'm fine." I said to assure him, if not myself.

He continued to look at me, "Take care of yourself, Ms. O'Conner and take this warning as seriously as it was intended."

After he left, I just sat there for a while thinking of all kinds of "I shoulds," and not doing any of them. I should call the glass place. I should try to clean up the paint. I should call Marti. But they all involved the biggest should of all— I should make myself go back into that house. Man, this detective stuff, in real life, isn't what it's cracked up to be. Or else, I'm a lot wimpier than paperback PI's.

I don't know how long I sat there stewing, and I also don't know how I finally got up the gumption to go back in the house, but I did. I called Michael's Glass Repair and they promised to send someone right over.

While waiting, I righted the chairs and the coffee table and then got out a pail of water and a scrub brush. I dumped some of the cold water out of the pail and started scrubbing. With the front door open and the screen door locked, I found I didn't feel so oppressed by the house. By the time I saw the truck with the yellow and blue Michael's logo on the side, the red stain was changing to pink in places.

I stood up to unlock the door and a pleasant looking man in his thirties stepped in.

"Hi, I'm Michael Anderson," he stopped abruptly and stood staring down at the splashes of red at his feet. "Wow, what happened?"

I told him about the breaking and entering and showed him the window. He took measurements and discussed various options with me. A replacement window would be ordered and could be here in several weeks. He then went back to his truck for wood and tools. Meanwhile, I took a few swipes with the scrub brush on the couch. It might be time to look for a new one, a couch with a clean slate.

I went back to work on the carpet as Michael and a helper cleaned up the old glass.

Then, while they pounded away, boarding up the window, I slunk into my office. What a mess. Each appraisal file is a couple of inches thick. I thought about it for a minute then decided to proceed slowly. If I was right, and also lucky, most of the papers belonging to any one file would be fairly close together.

I started into the pile, and, as it turned out, I was right. This wouldn't be an insurmountable task. But what would anyone have been looking for? As I worked, I came to the conclusion that it was probably just part of the whole scare tactic.

An hour or so later, Michael et al had left and the phone rang, startling me. Could it be the intruder, calling to see if I was home? I checked the caller ID. It was a Metro Detroit telephone number and one that I didn't know. That seemed safe so I picked up just before the caller would have been sent into voice mail.

Chapter Seventeen

"Hello?"

"Onalee? . . . What's wrong? This is Rick, um Rick Sommers. Is this a bad time?"

"Oh, hi Rick. No this is fine. I didn't recognize the phone number."

"It's my cell phone. Are you really okay? You don't sound like yourself."

"No, I'm fine," I said in a pseudo-perky tone. "Why are you calling me, when it's not the pre-dawn hours?"

"I'm in your area. I met with a client in Boyne City this afternoon and I'm just now heading into Petoskey. I was hoping we could get together. I would have called earlier but this just came up and I didn't know how long the meeting would take."

I considered a minute. Rick, here? I'd love to see him, but at any other time than this.

He broke into my thoughts. "Onalee? Listen, we can make it another time, I just wanted,"

"No, I can go," I blurted out. "I'd love to. But I need a little time. It's been an odd day."

"Not another body, I hope?"

"Um, no, not exactly. Anyway, we can talk about all that later. Want to meet at the Green Door? It's a great place for dinner."

"Sure. Give me directions and name a time."

*****

We agreed to meet at 5:00 p.m., which meant a whirlwind shower and primpathon for me. Other than the chaos inflicted by the intruder, the house didn't look too bad. Not that Rick was coming back here. But, just in case. Actually, I had to admit, the enforced action was much better than sitting around the house feeling sorry for myself.

Rick and I had known each other for years, but our friendship, at least until lately, had been limited to my early morning phone calls pumping him for market information and occasional times when we'd both attended the same real estate function. Over the past few months it had changed, and our conversations had gotten longer and more personal. I loved his sense of humor and he seemed to get a kick out of the stories of my appraisal escapades.

I knew he always went out of his way to help me, as well as a lot of other appraisers,

130

and that impressed me. The truth is, I did have a bit of a crush on him. I knew he'd been married once and divorced, but what I didn't know was, whether he was involved with anyone now.

In the looks category he is fairly average, just the way I like my men. My Mama always said, "There aren't that many really good looking men around and the ones that are, are usually full of themselves." I guess that isn't always true but the other problem, as I see it, with being a hunk-aphile is that there are always other women making plays for your man. Not being film star material myself, I didn't want the constant competition.

But getting back to Rick, I would guess he's about 5'10" and trim. His best feature is his eyes, which, if I were sixteen again and writing a diary, I would describe as limpid pools of root beer. But considering my age and professional demeanor, I shall herewith describe as large and brown. And maybe throw in "expressive", too.

I reached into my closet to grab my hottest jeans. No matter how chunky I am on any given day, these jeans somehow manage to make me look slender and willowy. I also snatched the sky blue tee shirt that has just the right amount of snugness.

I'm usually on the slim side, depending on the day. This is, naturally, thanks to jogging rather than any dietary restraint on my part. Gazing at myself, post shower, I was squeaky clean and, I had to admit, suitably fetching.

* * * * *

Rushing as I did, I managed to walk through the front door of the Green Door, by a very acceptable 5:20. A few early diners were scattered around but I quickly spotted Rick at a corner table. He waved to me and I saw two bottles of Molson Ice on the table in front of him.

Good man, he'd remembered my favorite brew. He stood up when I got to the table and gave me a friendly hug. Over dinner I caught up with his life during the past few weeks and filled him in on the investigation. When I told him about the intruder he became visibly upset.

After dinner we sat and talked over decaf coffees, then he suggested going for a walk by the water. I gave him his choice of the quiet beach by my house or the city park studded with boats, a baseball diamond and a bike path. Since he opted for the beach, we drove to my place and walked from there.

Strolling along the little path that leads from the bike path to the beach, Rick abruptly halted and gazed at the expanse of shimmering turquoise blue water in front of him. Turning to me, he said, almost reverently, "Onalee,

132

you are so lucky to live in such a beautiful spot. You've got to be glad you moved back, aren't you?"

"Yes," I said. "Though there was a sharp reduction in my income and that's even though I still travel to work around Detroit on occasion. Especially if it's to appraise a good old industrial building," I added.

"I know you love those industrial buildings. Have you managed to coerce anyone into letting you drive a fork lift yet?"

A grin spread over my face, "Sadly no. But," I turned towards the water and pumped my fist in the air, "tomorrow is another day and as God is my witness, I'll never give up trying."

"Then I say, good luck to you, Scarlet O'Praiser."

We stopped and took our shoes off so that we could scuff along, bare foot, through the sand, still warm from the evening sun. Rick began peppering me with questions about Petoskey stones. So, I gave him the usual canned speech that I give to the camper/tourists I encounter at the county park. "They're actually the fossil of a coral that lived here thousands of years ago when this area was beneath the sea. The best way to spot them is when they're wet and their markings show up, so it's easier to find them right down by the water."

"Do you think I can find one?"

"I don't know. I plant some every summer so that at least a few campers will hit the jackpot. Of course the ones I plant aren't the really good ones. I keep those for myself."

Laughing he grabbed my hand and pulled me toward the water's edge. "Come on. I want one for my desk."

We ambled along. Petoskey stones aren't as easy to find these days, not like they had been when I roamed up and down this beach as a kid. Then we'd find so many fistfuls, we couldn't carry them all back to our towels.

In those days I had thought that I might someday make my fortune with them. I still have most of the stones I'd found back then, but, their increasing scarcity hasn't driven the prices up as far as I'd hoped. So instead, I ply my trade as an appraiser, albeit, one blessed with shoeboxes brimming with Petoskey stones. At a guess, I could probably sell them all and gross a cool three figures, but I'll hang on to them. Who knows?

"Hey I just figured out something," I said to Rick. "I'll bet that intruder heard I had a small fortune in Petoskey stones tucked away at my house, and that was what he was searching for."

Hot Property

Rick was squatting, studying stones in an area of the shore dotted with small pebbles but he jerked his head up, glowering. "Don't joke about that. It's scary stuff, Onalee."

"Rick, I was just kidding. Come on."

"I know. I don't want to be a jerk, but that bothers me." He stood up, walked over to me and looked directly into my eyes.

"Yeah, me too, but I just wanted to give you some idea of the importance of Petoskey stones."

"Aghghghg," he said then leaned in and kissed me. My arms circled around him before I was even aware I was doing it. Within his hug, I felt relief. I hadn't realized I was so tense. I don't know how long we stood there, but we suddenly heard a family coming towards us. We disentangled and jumped a couple of feet apart to present a wholesome front to the two small children tripping towards us between their parents.

Our mutual jump struck us both as hopelessly corny and we started laughing so hard we could barely stand up straight. With an effort, we sobered up enough to say cheery hellos to the young couple as they passed by us, but then, looking at each other, we broke out laughing again. I couldn't be with a guy who didn't make me laugh.

"Enough of that folderol, we've got to find you a Petoskey stone, young man," I said.

Eventually I spotted one. It was perfect, the whole stone was covered with the hexagonal shapes that are distinctive of Petoskey stones and in this case, the marks were quite well defined. It would polish up beautifully.

"Here you go, Rick," I said handing it to him.

"Wow, Onalee, that's great," he said appreciatively.

"It's yours. Souvenir of our evening together."

"Thank you. I'll keep it and always think of you when I see it." He put it in his pocket and continued his search.

"You want to find one on your own don't you?"

He looked at me and grinned, "Yeah. At least if I can."

Ten or fifteen minutes later, I was getting a tad bored. I started looking harder myself and thought I saw one laying a couple of feet to his right. "Sometimes I've found that if you look higher up the beach you can find them. I guess maybe they've been overlooked up there," I called over to him.

"Oh yeah? I'll try that," he said and stepped to the right. The stone lay right in his path now but they are tough to spot when they're dry. Will he find it? Come on Rick. A lit-tle more to the right. That's it. You're looking right at it. Oh no. There he goes, stepping right over it. Geeshshsh.

"You know, Rick, sometimes I pour water over a bunch of dry stones so that the markings will stand out better. Want to try that?"

"Sure."

Unfortunately there is usually some litter on the beach and I spotted a paper cup I could fill with water. Under Rick's watchful eye, I poured it on a group of stones including, of course, the Petoskey stone.

"Is that one?" he asked, stooping down to pluck it off the sand.

"Well, lookie there. It is, and it's a good one too."

He stared intently at me, as if suspecting foul play, but didn't say anything. After admiring it, he stuffed it into his pocket. Then, we turned around and, holding hands, strolled back down the beach.

When we were on the quiet street behind my house, he turned to me and said, "Onalee. Listen. I don't want you to be alone tonight. I'm not. . . I mean, I'm planning to sleep on your couch. It's because of the break-in. I know I'd feel a little uncomfortable if I were you. At least the first night. Are you okay with that?"

I had been wondering what I was going to do. My house didn't seem safe anymore. "Oh Rick, that would be great. Thanks."

"There's one other little problem."

Uh oh. I was immediately on my guard. A married man palming himself off as a single guy? "What?" I asked with some trepidation.

"Well. I usually turn in around 9:00 or 9:30. Is that going to inconvenience you?"

Whew. "Oh geesh, no. Of course not. I'm an early to bed kind of girl myself. But," I stopped, gathering my courage, and turned to face him. "Um, I've got to know, Rick. Are you serious with anyone right now?"

He reached for my other hand, "I feel like I'm on the verge of getting very serious with someone. She's the hottest appraiser in Michigan."

* * * * *

The stillness of the moonless night was shattered by the opening chords of Beethoven's Fifth. My eyes popped open and I flicked the light on my bedside table. It was 5:00 a.m. and I could hear Rick talking softly in the living room. I walked over to the airbed where he was sitting up, bare-chested, holding a cell phone to his ear. My quilt loosely covered him from his hips down.

Hmnmnmn. I couldn't help but speculate. Did I, Onalee O'Conner, have Rick Sommers, world-famous (well, Detroit-famous broker) sitting, starkers, in my living room? Wait till I tell Marti.

I heard him chuckle. "I know that what I'm asking is next to impossible. But I'm not in the office now and don't have the information with me. So if you really need those comps you'll just have to get up before dawn tomorrow, too. You'll get a lot more accomplished and you'll thank me for this someday." He looked up at me and grinned. Oh how cool. He was talking to some other appraiser who had called him for comps. I grinned back, conspiratorially.

"Okay, Marti, talk with you in the morning. Bye."

My jaw dropped as Rick threw back the quilt.

Chapter Eighteen

Turns out he's a boxers kind of guy.

"Good morning, Onalee," he said, smiling. He stretched and climbed out of the air bed. "I hate to sleep and run, but I do need to get back to the Motor City."

"How about coffee and breakfast?"

"I never turn down a cup of coffee but if you don't mind, I'll take it for the road."

I scurried to the kitchen and turned on the coffee maker. Soon its life-giving aroma tinged the air. As I was pouring the dark elixir into his travel mug, I felt Rick's arms encircle me from behind. "Onalee, will you be okay now?"

I leaned my head against his shoulder. "Yeah. But thank you for staying last night. I wouldn't have wanted to be here alone."

"That's understandable. And thank you. I had a great time yesterday. I'll call you." He spun me around to face him and gave me a slow deep kiss. Then he zipped out the door.

Hot Property

"Drive carefully," I yelled after him. It was 5:15 a.m.

$$\star \star \star \star \star$$

I worked on my appraisal until 6:30 and then suited up for a run. It was a mild morning but mostly overcast and breezy. I zipped along the beach and fulfilled a rare urge to go an extra mile to the ice cold creek that empties into the lake. An hour later I made my way from the shore back up to the bike path. I was loping down the street towards my house, when I saw a crumpled figure up ahead. I gasped. As I closed the gap between us, she turned her anguished face towards me.

"Mrs. Stirnaman. Are you okay? What happened?"

"Oh, Onalee. . . . I'm so clumsy. I came out to put a letter in the mailbox . . . for our mail carrier to pick up and . . . and . . . . I seem to have fallen."

"Can I help you up?"

"Dear, I'm afraid I can't walk. I think I've really fixed myself up this time."

"I'd better call an ambulance then," I said, reaching into my pocket for my cell phone.

"Yes, I suppose that's best," she said with a sigh.

I put my quick call into the 9-1-1 dispatchers and then squatted down beside my neighbor and studied her. "Can I get you anything? A pillow or blanket? A glass of water?"

"No, help will be here soon. Thank you, Onalee. Oh, but, dear, I'll . . . I'll need my purse and my Medicare card. Could you run into my house and get them for me? Uh . . . oh." She'd shifted a bit, grunting as she did so. "It's upstairs in my . . . my bedroom closet."

She was clearly in pain but seemed to be stable. I'm no nurse but I didn't think she was exhibiting the classic signs of shock so I clambered to my feet and sped into her house. At the door I was almost knocked over by a very agitated Julian. I gave him a hasty pet on his head and bee-lined for the stairs. Julian maintained his post at the door where he could watch over his beloved dog-mom. I'd never been upstairs in this house but only one door was open and it was Mrs. Stirnaman's bedroom.

She had a number of purses hanging on pegs and I sorted through them and nabbed the one with her wallet. A siren cut through the morning air as I barreled back down to the first floor. Julian, pawing at the door, was now barking frantically as he watched the ambulance pull up near Mrs. Stirnaman.

142

"Good boy, Julian. Everything is going to be okay," I said and tried to pet him again. I don't think he even heard me. I gently pushed him aside, squeezed past and out the door. The paramedics were bent over Mrs. Stirnaman as I fidgeted nearby.

She glanced up and saw me hovering a few yards away. "I'm sorry, I don't know your surnames. Mr. Ralph and Mr. Mike, this is my darling neighbor, Miss Onalee O'Conner."

We exchanged hellos and the two men nodded at me but then snapped back to their patient. After what seemed like an hour but was probably just five or six minutes, they hoisted her on a gurney for transport in the ambulance. I handed her the purse. "Mrs. Stirnaman, is there anything else you need?"

"Onalee. Thank you so much. Would you mind looking after Julian until I'm back? He's had his breakfast and morning walk but he'll want his lunch at 12:00 sharp and his afternoon jaunt at 3:00. He likes dinner at 5:00 p.m., if I'm not back by then." The paramedics had stopped during this discussion but at a slight nod from Ralph they hefted the gurney into the back of the ambulance. Moments later it motored quietly along our street towards the hospital.

It was still awfully early so I showered and had a raspberry smoothie. Then, I sped over to the hospital.

Mrs. Stirnaman was having x-rays taken when I arrived. Shortly afterwards we both learned that she'd broken her hip. She was admitted and would have surgery the following day.

After seeing that Mrs. Stirnaman was settled in, I zipped back to the neighborhood, arriving at her house in time for the "12:00 sharp" lunch hour for Julian. When I got there I could see him in the front window waiting expectantly for his mistress's safe return. After I unlocked and opened the door he bounded over and looked up at me from under his eyebrows. Clearly he was a canine with questions. I knelt down and threw my arms around his chest. "Julian, sweetie, she's going to be fine. And so are you. I'm here to get your lunch and later you and I will go on a nice long walk together."

I got to my feet and found his bowl and food where Mrs. S. had told me they'd be. Julian heard the chinging notes of kibbles striking stainless steel but did not come over towards his food. In fact he turned and trotted back to his perch in the chair by the window. I picked up a couple of the tasty morsels and took them over to him, placing them right under his nose. He turned away. After that he even turned down my bribery of a slice of cheddar cheese.

I gave up but left his food in the kitchen where he could eat if he began to feel peckish

144

at a later time. He had a clean bowl with plenty of fresh water so reluctantly I said my good-byes and strolled back to my house.

After the disturbing events of this morning, I wasn't very hungry, either. I hopped aboard the computer. The particular appraisal I was working on was going smoothly, which happens so infrequently that it is cause for some concern.

On the other hand, it was a good thing, because my mind kept jitter-bugging around. First there were warm flashbacks of last night with Rick, then I'd think of poor Mrs. Stirnaman, then the break-in, which segued into ideas about the investigation. That's where I'd stop myself.

Hadn't I stuck my neck out too far already? All I had to show for it was a stained carpet and couch and a broken boarded up window. The thought that someone had just waltzed right in here and vandalized my house was more than a little disturbing.

Anyway, I had appraisals that were begging to be completed. With that I'd force my mind to refocus on my industrial building. But not for long. Even if I did quit trying to solve my whodunit, would the murderer back off? Maybe not, I might still be in danger.

I tapped the keys for a few more minutes. Actually, it was a whydunit wasn't it? If I could pinpoint the motive, it would go a long ways towards narrowing down my long list of suspects.

The way I saw it, the probable perps fell into two camps. Either Jonathon was killed because of his development debacle or it was due to his frequent episodes of extramarital escapades. Both had been risky behavior on Jonathon's part.

I worked for a little longer then decided it was a good time to take a bit of a break, and drive to the county courthouse to retrieve more information. I spent some time going through records in the Register of Deeds office and then toddled down the hall to the Equalization office. In Michigan, the Equalization Department, among other things, acts as the assessor for some of the small townships. I had heard through the grapevine that a building had sold in La Croix Township and I might be able to get the details from this department. I opened their frosted glass and metal door and stepped up to the counter.

"Hi Onalee. How's it going?"

"Hello Georgia. I'm looking for Jake. Is he in?"

"You're in luck. He's been out in the field a lot lately but he just stepped in. I'll get him."

A minute or so later he walked out from his office behind the reception area. "Uh oh. It's an appraiser. I'm on my way out," Jake said with a straight face.

"Oh no you don't, buster. My tax dollars say that you have to stay right here and help me."

He grinned, "How the heck are you, Onalee? Long time no see."

"I'm fine. But it has been a while. I just haven't been working on anything where I needed to call on any of your vast expertise."

"This calls for an even bigger uh-oh. This must be really nasty stuff you're going to ask me to do."

I explained what I needed and that sent Jake back into his office to search for a couple of files. As I stood cooling my heels, my mind reverted to the cast of suspects.

A voice broke into my musings, "You look lost in thought."

"Oh my gosh. Hello, Marissa. What are you doing here?"

"I need to get some information on one of my listings. How've you been?"

"Great. You?"

"Real good but this week has been crazy. And it's only Tuesday. Hey, feel like a bite

147

to eat after you're finished here? It's after one o'clock."

"Sure. That would be fun."

We both finished our research and then strolled out to the parking lot. "I'll drive, you drove last time," Marissa said.

*****

After some deliberation, we settled on a bar and restaurant in the middle of downtown Petoskey called the Park Garden. It's been around since about 1900. Today, like usual I gazed up at the old, pressed tin ceilings high above our heads. The bar, which is about thirty feet long and three feet wide, is made of a single slab of mahogany. Its rich dark wood gleams under the artificial lights.

There's even a resident ghost, living, well, maybe not exactly living, residing upstairs. A number of people who have worked there have sworn that they could hear him clomping around after hours when nobody else was there. Spooky.

Today there were people around and no sounds of ghostly footfalls as we threaded our way through the restaurant to a table towards the middle of the room. The other diners were mostly women, probably girlfriends getting together to have lunch and then "do" the stores afterwards.

Hot Property

Marissa ordered a hamburger and I opted for the house salad, including roasted pecans and dried cherries. She was in the middle of telling me a hilarious story about a recent showing she'd had, involving a pet skunk when a guy I knew, Rob Darnell, walked by our table. He is an English instructor at our local community college.

"Hi Rob," I said, catching his eye.

"Onalee. Hi, I didn't see you." Then he did a double take. "Well, and hello to you too, Marissa."

"How do you two know each other?" I asked, surprised. Petoskey isn't a large city but it seems like most people still tend to only know a fraction of the people living here.

"Marissa and I dated for a while. That is, until she dumped me."

"Biggest mistake I ever made, Rob," she said and treated him to her blazing smile.

"Yeah, right. I wish," he said, shaking his head. "Well, you ladies have a good day. I've got to get to my meeting in the back room. Great seeing you both." He hurried away accompanied by our chorus of good byes.

Just then our meals came and the conversation turned again to work and the rest of Marissa's "skunk from hell" story.

Afterwards we both ate contentedly for a bit, then she asked if I was keeping busy.

"Yes, but I haven't been spending enough time on my appraisals to make much headway. Other things keep happening."

She arched her eyebrows. "Oh. A new guy, perhaps?"

"Well, kind of. And then I got sort of involved in the murder, you know." I stabbed a dried cherry and popped it in my mouth.

"Involved? Other than finding the body?" She looked at me, quizzically. "You're not still playing Nancy Drew, are you?" She asked, and smiled.

"Not really. But, I am a suspect too, and if I can dig something up, then I could take the heat off myself."

"And have you? Dug anything up, I mean." She nibbled on a sweet potato chip.

Meanwhile, I was fishing around in my big salad bowl for more pecans and cherries, but I glanced up. "Not really. At least, I don't think so. But somebody must, because they broke into my house yesterday."

Marissa laid her half eaten chip down. "You're kidding. Were you there?"

I shook my head, "Fortunately, no."

"Did they steal anything?" She asked.

"No."

She cocked her head and looked at me. "Are you sure someone broke in?"

"Oh yeah. There was a broken window where they entered and they left my office in a shambles. Also, they spilled red paint all over, to make it look like blood, I guess."

"You poor thing. What did you do?"

"I called the police."

"Did they have any idea who did it? And why?"

"No. But Detective Costas said he thought it was a warning to me to quit meddling in the case."

She nodded her head. "That makes sense to me. Are you going to quit?"

"Well, I definitely thought I would yesterday. But, today, I'm having second thoughts. It's kind of grabbed hold of me."

"Then, you go, girl," she said and grinned. "But be careful. It sounds dangerous." She bit into her burger.

"I know. It does to me too, but I'll watch my back. Marissa, I know I've asked you this before, but who do you think did it?"

She laid down her burger, chewed for a bit and looked at me thoughtfully. "I don't know. Any one of a number of people."

151

"I interviewed Linda P.-Lorian yesterday."

"She's such a ho," Marissa snarled. I looked up sharply and she laughed. "Well bless your corn-fed eyeballs, Onalee. Haven't you ever called someone a ho? She gets on my last nerve. Anyway what did darling Linda have to say?"

"Not much. She isn't the friendliest person, is she?"

"Yes, about as friendly as a venomous adder. Anyway, I'm curious." She paused. "What did you think of their collection of trophy animals hanging on the walls. I'm a carnivore, and even I find it revolting."

"I talked with her at the tennis club, not her house. But what do you mean about the animal heads? Is Mike Lorian a big game hunter?"

"Uh huh. He apparently thinks it's a real studly thing to do. In fact I hear that Linda is also quite the sharp shooter now."

"What?"

"Oh, yeah," she said leaning in over the table and speaking in a lower voice. "What I heard is that our very own little Linda P.-Lorian has been taking shooting lessons over at the Rain Bow Range."

"Wow. No kidding." I said. "And as we both know, Jonathon Richmond was shot. Hmm. I thought . . . since women aren't usually so big on guns . . ."

"That it had probably been a guy?"

"Yeah," I said, musing.

"Well, maybe it was a guy. There's also the Great White Hunter Mike Lorian. And I still think, after it's all said and done, that the tree-hugging arsonist will turn out to be the one who did it." She took a small bite of her burger. "Anyway, let's get down to business. Who is this guy who has been keeping you so very occupied?"

"Well, I kind of hate to say. I don't think we're exactly an item yet."

Marissa grinned, "Come on, Onalee. I won't tell a soul. At least not till you tell me I can. Scout's honor," she wheedled.

"Oh, okay. It's Rick Sommers."

"The Rick Sommers. From Detroit?"

"Yup."

"Whoa," she said and sat back in her chair. At least you don't have to worry about him keeping you out too late."

We both chuckled. "Do you know him very well?" I asked.

"Not too well. Of course we all know about his habit of getting into the office at three a.m. That's just crazy, if you ask me. Anyway,

I've done a couple of deals with him but that was, of course before I moved up here." She looked thoughtful. "Rick Sommers. . . He always seemed like a really nice guy even if he has practically cornered the Detroit real estate market. Rick Sommers, my, my, my. You don't mess around, girl. Can I at least tell Henry and Ted, back at the office? They know him, too."

"No. You promised."

"Pretty please? I'll give you a juicy tidbit of gossip."

"No. But, what's the gossip?"

"You know it doesn't work that way. It's about Amber. Amber Czinski," she said in a sing-songy voice.

"Amber. About the case?"

"Could be."

"Okay, tell you what. If Rick calls me again to go out with him, I promise I'll call you and you can tell your homies. At least as long as you don't exaggerate the importance of it."

"Do you promise to put me on your speed dial and call me first?"

"Yes. Now tell me." It was now my turn to wheedle.

"Okay." she chuckled. "Especially since I would have, anyway. Then again, it probably doesn't mean anything."

"Tell me," I growled.

"Okay, here goes. Our dear Susie Secretary or Felicity File and F--- Me. I'll leave it up to you to fill in the blank there. Anyway, she up and quit. In fact it was the day after you two had your little chat."

"Really. Did she say why?"

"No, although, my guess would be that the fringe benefits aren't as good now. But then, I'm probably a bit jaded." She picked up her purse and pawed through it. Then she continued, "I did hear though, that Linda P. was trying to get her fired, so maybe she knew her days were numbered."

"Is she still around town?"

"I have no idea. I can't begin to tell you how little interest I have in her."

"Ooookay. I just might try to track her down."

She finally extracted her keys, "Be careful, Onalee. You need to keep yourself healthy for Rickie Baby."

"Would you ladies like to see the dessert cart?" The server asked as she cleared away our plates. We both passed and got up to leave.

155

After Marissa dropped me off at my car I just sat there going over all of her revelations. Amber gone, and right after I had talked with her. I wondered if she knows where I live. She seemed capable of vindictive behavior.

Zinski, I needed to remember her last name. Then there was also Linda P. and Mike Lorian. I sure would never have taken Linda for the Annie Oakley type, but what did I know?

Chapter Nineteen

I drove home in a mental fog, rehashing
everything I knew. Pulling into the driveway,
I parked and sat. I knew what the problem was.
I didn't relish the idea of going through that
front door and possibly finding something else
awry.

Get over it, I scolded myself, and eased
out of the car. I slowly unlocked my front
door, opened it, and keeping most of my body
safely outside, cranked my neck around the
door-frame, and into the house.

The paint stain was right where I had left
it. The boarded up window was keeping my
dining room in gloom, but nothing seemed
different from this morning. I stepped all the
way in. Everything looked secure, but it
didn't feel safe. Would it ever?

In the kitchen, I poured a big glass of
water, drank part of it and then proceeded to
the office. Things were still in disarray but
I had gotten the area around my desk mostly
straightened up. I sat down and began to type,
but my mind kept drifting off. The subject
property has a gross building area of . . .

hmmm . . . I wonder if I could interview Linda Lorian's gun class instructor.

Finally I gave in, grabbed the phone and punched in the number for the Rain Bow Range. I reached a recording telling me that the Women's gun class scheduled for June 18th was going to be held, weather permitting, at 3:00 p.m. Then it said that it was an ongoing class and beginners were always welcome. Wow, that was an hour from now. I could get Julian out, a bit early, for his 3:00 walk and then drive down there.

By now it had warmed up to about 80 degrees. A soft breeze drifted through the cloudless sky.

Poor Julian was still in the window, his bowl beside him, untouched. I attached a leash to his collar, grabbed several poop bags from the hallway stash and we were off. We strolled down my street to the bike path, moving to the side of the road when cars passed by. The only thing my perfect little neighborhood lacked was sidewalks. But, traffic was usually light. Julian stopped only a couple of times for potty breaks. I had walked him a few times in the past and this was just not like him. He walked by even his favorite bushes without a backward sniff.

Since Memorial Day, the herds of tourists had grown as we fell deeper and deeper into summer. Bicyclists, singly and in groups, sped

along the bike path and so I kept Julian close
beside me on a short leash as we stepped
along. A lone kayaker kept pace with us just
off shore in the aqua waters of the bay. A
mid-afternoon dog walk is the perfect break.

* * * * *

Thirty minutes later I wheeled along US-131,
by-passing downtown Petoskey then proceeding
south toward Walloon Lake. I turned east, then
south again on Howard Road, and pulled into
the gravel parking lot of the Rain Bow Range.
Nine or ten other cars were parked in the lot,
including an impossibly cute, yellow
convertible Mini Cooper. That car, or one
exactly like it, had been parked outside the
tennis club.

Stepping out of my car I noticed a small
white wood-sided building that could use a
coat of paint. The shooting range was behind
it. I walked around the building and saw a
cluster of women chattering and grouped around
a card table. It looked like a meeting of a
middle-aged ladies' book club.

Off a bit by herself and striking a haughty
pose stood Linda P-Lorian. Her eyes flicked
over me, then narrowed. If looks could kill,
Linda P. wouldn't be wasting any of her
bullets on me. She abruptly turned and stalked
still farther away from the rest of the women.

That's exactly what you'd expect from a ho. With a toss of my head, I made my way up to the small knot of women.

There was a sign-up sheet and a man watching over it. At the table, I picked up an entry form and filled in my name. I had to show my driver's license as well, to a man who identified himself as Bob Golden. He was a bit pudgy and looked to be about sixty years old. I was the last one to arrive, as it was by now a little after 3:00. Bob also signed me up for a rental gun for the class.

"Okay, ladies. Those of you who are renting firearms, come into the office and pick up your guns and paraphernalia."

Like colorful ducklings, we fell into line behind Bob and entered the small building. He handed me a twenty-two caliber revolver, a plastic box of bullets, safety glasses and ear protection.

"Okay? Everybody all set?" Bob asked.

We all nodded and he shepherded us back out the door and into the sunshine. About a hundred yards beyond the table was a shooting range set up with paper targets on wooden boards. The targets were the dark shape of a man's head and torso.

"Remember, ladies, only point your guns down range. And this wooden counter?" He

160

patted the wooden divider in front of all of us. "Never step in front of it."

As the women started shooting, Bob sauntered over to me. "You're the only beginner today, so I'll be a little brief, but I want you to stay after class for a few minutes while we go over some rules and laws."

Bang! Even with my ear protection, I jumped at the report of a particularly large weapon to my right. I scanned down the line of women and saw Linda P. leveling a monster-sized pistol at her target. Bang!

Bob followed my gaze.

"What kind of gun is that?" I asked, pointing in Linda's direction.

"Today she's shooting a .357 Magnum. Loud, isn't it?" He then carefully showed me how to load my revolver and how to hold the gun, using both hands. "You'll barely feel a kick when you shoot this gun, so it's a good one to start off with."

The tiny gun was cute, I had to admit. I fired off a few rounds, but my paper victim failed to feel the sting of my bullets. Bob, standing beside me, gave me a few more pointers. We squeezed off more rounds until the air was filled with the acrid smell of gun smoke. Then Bob issued a cease-fire.

Connie Doherty

"Okay, ladies. Let's look at everyone's results. Lisa. Well done. You're much more consistent than last week. Monica, you need to steady your arm a bit but I see a lot of improvement from you too." He went down the line criticizing and encouraging. Then he got to Linda P. "Linda. As I always tell you, you have a real knack for this. Such a tight grouping. Excellent." I watched her simper a bit while he continued on to the last two women in our group. Mercifully, he didn't critique me.

"Now Sara tells me that she brought us all a batch of fresh baked oatmeal cookies and a big ole jug of ice-cold lemonade, so I'd say it's break time." Smiles broke out around the group. We laid our arms on the wooden counter, and scurried back to the little building. The cookies were still warm from the oven and chewy. The lemonade was cold, though a tad too tangy, in this food critic's humble opinion, to act as a suitable accompaniment to the oatmeal cookies.

I eavesdropped as Sara and several of the other women conversed about the cookies. Then their discussion turned to a luscious sounding recipe involving peanut butter and copious quantities of chocolate. It struck me that if I were to continue down this path to becoming a full-fledged, pistol packing gunsel, I'd better also sign up for Weight-Watchers or Over Eaters Anonymous.

162

Meanwhile, off to the side, Linda, who had eschewed any of the fattening snacks, was talking earnestly with Bob. Even from a distance, I saw him glowing with delight from her attention. Just as I was reaching for my third, well, okay, fourth, cookie, Bob called us back to class. Linda was already heading out the door and there was no chance of my catching her before we started, so instead I took my time and fully savored my last cookie.

Back at the range, we got new paper people to perforate and the shooting commenced. I did better this time, leading me to speculate about a possible connection between cookie consumption and gunplay. This time when Bob critiqued everyone, I was also praised as being "much improved."

Bob wrapped up the class, we tore down our targets and carried our guns and ammunition back to the building. Everyone was dismissed but me.

"Onalee, let's go over the regs. It's essential to know them where hand guns are concerned." He went over my obligations under the law and tested me on my knowledge of loading the revolver. "You're doing well, Onalee. Will we see you back here next week?" he asked as we walked out of the building.

"Yes. I think so. I enjoyed it," I said, then ventured, "Bob, has most of this class been coming for a long time?"

"Some of the ladies have, and as you can see, it's almost like a club for them." He leaned against the side of the building and folded his arms before continuing, "Then again, there are others, such as yourself, who are pretty new and inexperienced. I've been trying to talk a couple of the advanced students into going to some competitions."

"Really? Who?" I asked, hoping to sound innocent though he'd stepped right into my little verbal trap.

"Um, Linda and Karen are both real sharp shooters and I know they could do well."

"How long have they been coming?"

He rubbed his chin and thought a moment, "Oh, let me see. I'd say at least a year."

"Do you think they will compete?" I asked.

"As a matter of fact, I was talking with Linda about it today at break time. She tells me that she'd love to, later on, but the timing of the tournament, coming up in a couple of weeks, is bad for her. I don't think Karen will ever want to. That is, unless we host an event in Northern Michigan. She doesn't like to travel."

"Why do most people sign up for this class?"

"Well, why did you?"

"Um, I had a break-in recently and that got me thinking it might be a good idea to learn how to protect myself."

"That's the same with a lot of your classmates."

"And the two sharp-shooters?"

He eyed me before answering, "Karen lives way out in the boonies by herself. I think she worries a lot about personal safety. Linda? She and her husband go out west and, I think even to Africa, on hunting trips."

"I see," I said as we started walking toward our cars. "Bob, thanks for everything and I'll see you next week for sure."

It was going on 4:30 p.m. as I drove back into Petoskey. With a belly full of oatmeal cookies it suddenly seemed like a good idea to delve into the current whereabouts of the woman formerly known as Susie Secretary. If I was lucky, I might be able to track her down through the phone book.

As I pulled into my drive a dark sedan eased in right behind me.

Chapter Twenty

Trapped. Why hadn't I been paying attention to vehicles tailing me? Fear gripped my stomach, as my fingers flew to the automatic door locks. I flipped on the ignition key, hoping to raise my driver's side window, as Detective Costas ambled up to the car.

"Hello, there, Ms. O'Conner." Leaning into my still open window, his upper body cast a shadow over me.

"Um, hi." I said, looking up at him.

"Are you holding up okay after your break-in?" He looked at me intently.

Returning his gaze, I saw that today his eyes were pure Alaskan sled dog blue. "I'm fine. Thank you, Detective," I said in a clipped manner.

"Good. Even though no one was hurt, it was still a break-in and you should consider it a warning. Though I guess you do. I see you've gotten yourself a body guard."

"What?"

"I was in the Green Door the night of your break-in and was pretty surprised to see you out and about after such a traumatic day. But, then I saw that you had some muscle with you."

"Oh. That was a friend from downstate. I'm sorry. I didn't notice you at the restaurant."

"I was with a couple of other guys," he said. Looking away, he muttered, "Sometimes I get tired of my own cooking." Then turning his head back to face me he said, "Does your 'friend' know that you've been sticking your nose into a murder investigation?"

"He knows I found a body and had the break-in. That's about all it amounts to anyway." I turned away from him and pulled my keys out of the ignition.

"Oh? Why does the word on the street say that you're going around to other suspects and pumping them for information?"

My head swung back toward him, "Who told you that?"

"I have lots of sources. You know, I actually do this for a living. Have you ever heard the term, 'obstruction of justice'?"

"Yes, I have," I said, curtly.

"If you continue your interference, I will haul you in and allow you to experience, first hand, life in the Emmet County jail. Now, tell me your whereabouts today so far."

"It was another boring day. I'm appraising an industrial building in Charlevoix and I have a tight deadline. In fact, I really should get into my office right now, and work on it. So, if you'll excuse me," as I reached for the door handle, he stepped back.

"You get the broken window secured?"

"Yes."

"Do you feel safe enough going into your house now, or will your 'friend' be in there?"

"He had to go back to Detroit. But I'm fine, thank you, Detective," I said striving for my typical cool, professional demeanor. I walked to my front door and unlocked it. Before stepping inside, I looked back. Costas was standing there watching me. Then, he turned and strode back to his car. What was that all about? I thought he'd never leave and I had detective work to do. Getting back to Amber, the secretary.

My house looked exactly like it had before I left for the shooting range. It was still in disarray but apparently no new strangers had come in. I went over to my phone book and flipped to the Z section. I tried Zinski. Nada. Then, it must start with a C or an S. There were no Cinskis or Cinskeys. There were three Sinskies but they were Roger, J, and Paul and Sandra. I gave up, called R and L and asked for another broker I know who works there. "Hi, Henry. This is Onalee O'Conner," I said when he came on the line.

"Hello. How's it going?"

"Good. I wonder if you could do me a big favor. I'm trying to get in touch with Amber and I don't have her phone number or address. I'd purchased some Mary Kaye cosmetics from her and would like to pick them up. But, please keep that to yourself. I don't think she was supposed to be doing that on company time."

"Really? I didn't know she was into that. Let me put you on hold a sec and I'll try to find out for you."

He came back on the line with both a phone number and an address. Thinking I might learn more face to face, I planned to drive to her place. A condo project should be safe. There would be plenty of people around. Just then the phone rang and it was Rick.

"Hi, Onalee. You know, all the way back down to Detroit I was thinking about you."

"I thought about you today too, Rick." I heard a smile in my voice. "Last night was fun."

"It was and I already miss you. But, that's not exactly what I mean. You're done with your sleuthing around aren't you? I'm worried," he said, his voice edged with concern.

"Pretty much. You know deadlines. I've got to get some appraising done and forget the distractions. I chattered on, hoping to allay his fears.

"Onalee. Quit trying to change the subject. Tell me the truth. Are you still scouring the countryside, trying to track down the murderer?"

"Well, um. . . "

"You are, aren't you," he accused.

"Sort of, I said. "But it's kind of on the back burner now."

"Didn't that warning mean anything to you?"

"Of course, but guess what, Rick? Turns out Linda P. and Mike Lorian are both big game hunters. Did you know that?"

"So you are back at it and now you're nosing around people who not only have guns but know how to shoot them. I can't believe you. You need to stop this right now, Onalee."

"Quit telling me what to do."

"I'll quit all right," he shouted. "I'm done talking to you. Good bye."

He hung up. What nerve. I was shaking I was so furious. Who did he think he was, ordering me around? This was going to go down as the shortest-lived relationship on record. Geesh.

I grabbed my keys and headed to the front door. The phone was ringing as I closed it. No doubt it was Rick desperately needing to apologize and set things right. Well, he'd just have to wait and stew in his own juices, until I was available and had given sufficient thought as to whether I should accept it. Meanwhile the "hottest appraiser in Michigan" was, once again, on the case and off on the chase.

On the drive over to Amber's, I occupied my mind by trying to think of a way to convince the girl to let me talk to her again.

I pulled into the parking lot alongside the building. It consisted of ten townhouse style units that were actually condominiums. At a guess, I figured they'd fetch about $300,000, apiece. I wondered if Amber was renting one or if this had been, yet another, perk from R & L. I doubt that she had been paid enough to purchase one. I'd have to remember to go online and search the public records to check on the legal owner of this property.

Meanwhile, Amber's screen door was open and I could hear her radio blaring. From the sound of her taste in music, she wouldn't be accompanying me to the opera anytime soon. I knocked hard but she apparently couldn't hear me over Black Ice, or whoever was rapping on the airwaves. I tried the handle and the door opened. Amber really should be more careful, I was saying to myself as I caught sight of three long, painted nails, poking out from behind her leather couch.

Chapter Twenty-one

The fingers were still. Maybe she had gotten drunk and passed out. Or had fallen. My eyes frantically searched the room, but I didn't see anyone, lurking in the shadows. Creeping forward forced me to put more distance between myself and the front door.

"Amber!" I croaked as loudly as my hoarse voice allowed. Standing in front of the couch now, I could see all of her. Definitely dead. No need to touch the throat for vital signs. Her eyes were wide open in alarm. Her mouth formed an "O", as if her last act on earth had been a scream. But the only scream I heard now was my own.

I tore out of the condo and into the late afternoon sunshine. Several units down from Amber's, a man and a woman were sitting on their front porch. The man, who was looking at me, got to his feet.

"Is something wrong, young lady?" He walked over to me as I stood on the sidewalk and placed my call to 9-1-1.

Apparently he and his wife had just started to observe cocktail hour and after I finished my call, he tried to get me to drink a martini with them. I guess it was a nice gesture but it was the last thing on earth I wanted right then. I walked over with him to where his wife sat, watching us. After filling them in on what had happened, I asked if they had heard or seen anything. They'd been gone most of the day on errands and had heard nothing. Trying to normalize the situation, they tried to make small talk until the police arrived.

When I heard the sirens I dashed back to Amber's condo. There were three police cars and an ambulance. Several of the police went inside, while others cordoned off the area with crime tape. I sat on a nearby bench and waited. It wasn't long before a uniformed officer came over to me. "Are you the person who called 9-1-1?"

"Yes."

His eyes narrowed. "You look familiar. What's your name?"

I told him and he looked harder at me. "Have you, by any chance, found any other bodies recently?"

"She has. Seems she's picked up a new hobby." A too familiar voice emanated from behind the officer.

"Hi, Camille. She's the one who found the body," the officer said.

Camille? I'd been staring at the ground but my head jerked up and caught Costas' eye.

He held my gaze. "I figured as much. I'll take over from here, Jerry. Thanks." He turned back towards me and his eyes were the cold blue I'd remembered from our first encounter.

"This is your idea of a 'dead line' Ms. O'Conner?"

"Well. I had heard that Amber might be leaving town and I wanted to say good bye," I said.

"You two were friends?"

"I didn't know her well but I was sorry to hear she'd lost her job. I just wanted her to know that. . . That's not true. I was going to try to ask her some questions. And now . . . she's dead. You're right. I shouldn't be playing Kinsey Millhone."

He took several strides towards me and towered over me. His voice rose in pitch until he was yelling at me. "She lost her job? How did you know that?"

Cringing, I said, "Marissa Martin told me."

"When did she tell you this?"

"Earlier today."

"So you hot footed it right over here. Was she alive when you got here?" He was still yelling.

174

"No." I looked up into his angry eyes. "Wait a minute. You don't think I killed her, do you?"

"Oh no, Ms. O'Conner." This was delivered in a chilled monotone. "There are actually quite a number of our esteemed citizens tripping over dead bodies on any given day." Then his voice rose again, "Why in the world should I be suspicious of someone who has turned up at the scene of every violent crime that has been committed in Northern Michigan this summer? Anyone can tell you're just a civic-minded do-gooder."

I could feel tears welling up in my eyes. I tried willing them not to spill over. One started rolling down my cheek, so I quickly turned away. Sadness, mixed with guilt washed over me. I hadn't much cared for Amber, but she was only in her twenties. Her whole life had been ahead of her.

"You can cry all you want. But a young woman is lying in there dead and I intend to get to the bottom of it. Starting with you. Now, fill me in on every single detail of your day, and you better believe I'll fact-check everything."

I told him all I knew. At first I left out the part about the shooting range but later went back and filled that in.

"You weren't going to tell me you went to the Rain Bow, were you?" he said in an accusing tone.

"Yes, but I thought I should save that for last for the greatest impact."

He shook his head in disgust and then his eyes bored into mine again. "You know, at first, I have to admit, I thought you were kind of cute. But you've turned into a real pain in the butt. Not to mention that, at this point . . ." He jabbed his finger in the air at me, "you are, far and away, my number one suspect. For both this murder and the killing of Jonathon Richmond. Don't even think of leaving town, Ms. O'Conner. And, I wouldn't get too booked up with appraisals. That is, unless you can pound them out behind bars." He turned on his heel and stalked away.

"Detective Costas?"

"What."

"Can I go now?"

"By all means. But like I said, don't leave town. And you might want to call your lawyer."

I rose slowly to my feet. I hadn't noticed before, but a small crowd of people had gathered. They all stared at me as I stumbled past them to my car. Lawyer? Gees. How do you even know who to call? Should I look in the yellow pages?

Hot Property

Somehow I arrived home but I don't remember anything about the drive. I unlocked my door. The house was stuffy because I'd left all the windows closed up and locked, though it appeared that no one had bothered to break in, this time. I threw my purse on the couch and slunk towards my bedroom. Maybe I could just stay here until morning. Or next month, when all of this would just be a bad memory.

Julian flashed across my mind, and I looked at my watch. It was six o'clock and already an hour past his dinnertime. Besides, he should stay with me until Mrs. Stirnaman gets home, whenever that would be. I plodded back to her house where nothing had changed. The poor dog was still at his post at the window, and his lunch was untouched.

Knowing Mrs. S, Julian would have his own, comfortable dog bed and he would need it to feel at home at my house. I found one beside her bed plus another one in the kitchen. Well-loved stuffed animals were strew throughout the house. I grabbed Julian's bag of kibbles, the two beds, a couple of his toys, the food dish and water bowl and staggered back to my house. Then I went back and fetched Julian and another armful of his toys.

*****

I must have dozed off because the next time I looked at my clock it was 8:30 p.m. Somehow I'd managed to break up with a guy I had just started to get close to, learned how to shoot a gun, acquired a dog-boarder, and found a dead body, all in one day. No wonder I'd needed a nap.

I lay there, wondering if I should get something for dinner. The thought of food was almost enough to make me sick. Maybe after I joined Weight Watchers, I could start a new chapter. I would call it Body Finders Xtreme Diet. It would be at least as effective as a gastro bypass.

My phone started ringing and I dragged myself up. It was Marti. Should I answer it? I wasn't sure my voice would even work. Then again, I really needed to hear a friendly voice.

"Hello?"

"Onalee. Are you okay?"

"Just ducky." I said, sounding raspy even to my ears.

"What's going on?"

We spent the next hour talking and I began to feel a little better. She said she couldn't come up for awhile and asked if I wanted to come down and stay with her.

"I'm not supposed to leave town. Costas says I'm his number one suspect."

"Oooh, that means that the heat will be off Frank then."

"Gees, Marti. Thanks for your support."

"Oh, come on, On. You know that they'll figure out you're innocent. Eventually. But Frank did have a motive because of the condos. I'm worried about him. Even though there is no question of his innocence," she quickly added.

As we talked, a thought crossed my mind. "Marti, I ran into the nicest guy, today. He's a real hunk and he's available. His name is Rob Darnell."

"Are you thinking of dumping Rick Sommers for this man?"

"No, but he'd be a great guy for you."

"Why is he available if he's such a hot potato?"

"He was going out with a broker I know, named Marissa Martin but she dumped him."

"First of all, if he's not good enough for her, he's not good enough for me. Secondly, Rob? Robby? You know, I've never liked that name. And lastly, I already happen to have a great boyfriend named Frank. Don't try to palm off any other guys on me, On."

I sighed. "Okay, I tried." We talked for a little longer and then signed off. It was time to take Julian out.

"Julian, are you ready for a nightly stroll?" He raised his head from his paws, and gave me a quizzical look. "What I mean is, want to go for a walk?"

Now I was talking his language. He got to his feet and ambled over. The poor boy had been forlorn ever since I'd brought him here. He'd paced around the house, and he still hadn't touched his lunch. He'd finally found one of his beds and settled himself in it. A walk was bound to brighten his outlook on life.

Moments later Julian, with me in tow approached Mrs. Stirnaman's house. Straining at his leash, the dog raced past the bushes lining the walkway. He got to the front door exactly one taut leash-length ahead of me and began pawing frantically at it and mewing. When I reached his side, Julian looked over at me expectantly. "Julian, Maybelle gone," I told him.

I twisted the doorknob and pushed on the door to demonstrate for him. He let out a long moan and pawed at the door again. "Julian. Come. We've got sights to see and spots to sniff." I pulled on his leash and took him back to the road. His tail drooping, he trudged several paces ahead of me, not noticing any of his favorite trees or bushes.

Later that night, he wandered aimlessly around the house again as I performed my ablutions. I had placed Julian's largest bed beside my own and, giving him a hug, I told him to go to bed. Then I hopped into my own bunk. He circled the house one more time then settled into his nest. At nearly 10:00 p.m., on this June evening, it was still light outside. I fell asleep almost immediately.

Chapter Twenty-two

After a restless, nightmare strewn night, I awoke before six. I probably should run, I thought, but the idea was unappealing. Snap out of it, you big baby, I chided and forced myself into my running togs and shoes.

Julian and I would jog together. We started down the street towards the county park on opposite ends of a long leash. As we passed by Mrs. Stirnaman's house, Julian swung his head around but did not try to go down the walkway and kept up his pace. We stopped at a number of bushes and I waited as he sniffed, then left his mark.

We ran along the bike path, stopping about every twenty feet or so. After we got off the walkway and on to the beach, I unsnapped Julian's leash. At Mrs. Stirnaman's urging, I had done this before to allow Julian the freedom to run and be a dog. The run was good for both of us, and I was glad I had made the effort.

As I showered, I planned my day. For the first time in what seemed like ages, I would devote the entire day to appraising. I would finish the Charlevoix industrial building appraisal and ship it off. Then I would do some groundwork on that Plymouth property outside Detroit.

Shoot, that means I'll need to talk to Rick about sales. I didn't want to be the first one to call. Especially since I'd have to ask him for help. Oh well, I'd worry about that later. If nothing else, yesterday had taught me that a lot can change in one day.

I sat in front of my computer all morning, making great strides on the appraisal. It was a good thing because the bank emailed me to say that they had expected the report two days ago.

I had a quick lunch consisting of my usual bran cereal and yogurt, with a handful of peanuts on the side. Julian ambled over to his food dish and ate his kibbles. Finally, he got some food in his stomach. Meanwhile, his beloved Mrs. Stirnaman should be out of her surgery soon. I hoped everything had gone well for her. I planned to stop by the hospital later in the day.

Righteously, I went straight back to work. At about 1:30, the phone rang. The caller ID said, "private caller". Curious, I decided to pick up. It was Janet Richmond. So much for keeping my nose out of the investigation.

"Onalee. Are you okay? I heard you found another body. Can that be true?" she asked incredulously.

"Hi, Janet. Yeah, it's true but I'm fine. How did you hear about it?"

"From the office. Henry Greenley filled me in. Apparently you had called him to find out where Amber lived?"

"Yeah. Great timing, on my part, eh? Then again, the good news for you is, I guess I replaced you as the number one suspect."

"Oh, Onalee. I'm sorry," she paused. "Have you any idea yet, who did it?"

Why was she asking me this? The hairs on the back of my neck stood up. "No. I don't know any more than before," I said warily. "Have you figured out anything?"

"Listen, I need to take Lucas out. Feel like a walk? We could meet again at the nature center."

"Um, I don't know. I think I should just stick to appraising and keep my nose out of this."

"You're in it up to your eyeballs, Onalee. I'd think you'd at least want to clear your name."

"I need to finish this report. What if you come out here and we could walk around my neighborhood?"

184

She sighed, "Onalee, I didn't do it, if that's what you're afraid of. Besides, there should be plenty of other people at the nature center this time of day; so we wouldn't be alone in the woods. Luke needs to be able to run, not just trot around your neighborhood on the end of his leash. So, what do you say, thirty minutes?"

She hadn't struck me as a murderer. But could you really tell? A lot of people did walk their dogs at the nature center and Julian would possibly protect me. Besides there were usually joggers and other walkers there as well. It should be safe.

"I'm dog-sitting for my neighbor's golden retriever. Do you think the two dogs will get along? He needs a walk, too."

"If he's usually friendly with other dogs, I would think so. Why don't you bring him?"

"Okay. Thirty minutes, see you then."

We hung up. I typed for another twenty minutes, grabbed my keys and Julian and drove to meet Janet. I pulled into the parking lot at precisely 2:05. I smiled bitterly at the realization that I was on time, perhaps for the first time in my life. People had always told me the old line that I'd be late for my own funeral. The way things were going, maybe I'd prove them wrong.

Chapter Twenty-three

There were two other cars in the small gravel parking area. One was probably Janet's, but I wasn't sure what she drove. I'd been hoping for a full lot. I felt in my pocket. My thirty-seven blade Swiss Army knife formed a reassuring lump. Depending on how this scene played out and given the element of surprise, I could either stab Janet, open a bottle of wine for her, or pick my teeth.

I stepped out of my car as her big, reddish-gold dog bounded up. He was thrilled to see me, and, considering the rate at which I was now losing friends, that made him a welcome sight. Janet, near the trailhead, waved to me. She couldn't possibly be cold hearted enough to shoot me in plain sight of her beloved dog, could she?

I opened my back door and Julian jumped out. The two dogs sniffed each other, circling, tails wagging. Then Julian tore off with Lucas in hot pursuit. Lucas overtook Julian and they tumbled to the ground, growling and mouthing each other. Oh no, a dog fight. I chased after them.

"Onalee. It's okay. They're just playing. In fact, they're having a great time."

I stopped. "Really? It sounds pretty scary with all of that growling."

She laughed. "I know, but look at them now."

They had both rolled over onto their stomachs and were eyeing each other, panting. I guess it was break time. I ambled over to where Janet stood, watching the two dogs. We said our hellos and started down the path. I was relieved to see that she didn't mind taking the lead. We walked in silence for several minutes and were getting deeper and deeper into the forest when Janet abruptly turned back to me.

"Onalee. I needed to talk to you. Something happened today. I went to the office to pick up some of Jonathon's things. I'd heard that the office was closed today, because of Amber's death, so I figured this would be a good time." She started walking again. "I could go there and get in and out without having to hear a lot of sympathy from the staff. I know they'd mean well but I don't feel comfortable with it. When I pulled into the lot, there were a couple of other cars there. But, I'd come this far and I just wanted to get it over with."

She took a deep breath and continued, "As soon as I entered the building, I heard voices in the offices behind the lobby door. It was two people arguing." Stopping, Janet turned to face me again. "I didn't know what to do. Then I realized it was Mike and Linda P.-Lorian. I heard Michael say something like, I saw the way you two looked at each other. I'm not an idiot. Then Linda screamed, 'Go ahead and divorce me. I'll take you for everything you've got.' I stood there, torn between wanting to hear more and being afraid I'd get caught listening.

"I heard the sounds of a scuffle and got even more scared. Then, Mike burst through the door. Onalee, you know how his hair is always perfectly styled? Well, today it was sticking up all over his head. His lip was bleeding and his face was beet red. He screeched to a halt when he saw me and we just stared at each other. You know how his one eye twitches sometimes? I was afraid it was going to jump out of its socket. I guess neither of us knew what to say. Besides, he was breathing so hard, I was afraid he'd have a heart attack. Then he stumbled past me, threw open the front door and ran out."

I stood there, rapt, listening to Janet's amazing story. Was it the truth? It sure sounded convincing, but I watched her closely for any body language that might indicate she was lying.

188

She continued, "As I heard his car roar off, Linda charged into the room. As soon as she caught sight of me, she snarled, 'What the hell are you doing here?'

"I don't know why I answered her, but I was still so taken aback, she put me on the defensive. 'I just came to pick up some of Jon's things,' I said. 'I didn't realize you'd be here.'

"'I imagine you're going to make a shrine to your saintly husband,' she said and laughed. 'Now that our dear Amber is dead, too, don't you think they ought to be buried next to each other? That way they can roast in hell, entwined together.'

"I must have been staring at her because then she said, 'Oh don't give me that, I'm meek as a little mouse wifey and I'll stand by my husband because he was such a great man stuff with me. I know your kind. You were too scared to divorce him and try to make it on your own. Instead you just settled for the crumbs that other women, better than you, left of him.'

"This last part she screamed at me, then she said, 'Well, come to think of it, Amber the Idiot probably wasn't any better than you, but most of his other women were.' With that she deliberately walked fast and hard, right at me and knocked me down. Then she stomped out of the building. I sat there on the floor,

189

too stunned to move for a while. Eventually I got up and went home. I never did get Jon's things, and I still feel a little shaky."

She finished and now it was my turn to stare, openmouthed, at her. "Wow, Janet. That's terrible. You poor thing." I noticed her eyes were glistening.

"How could Jonathon have been with . . . with someone like that?" The floodgates opened and she sobbed. Troubled, Lucas went to her and nuzzled her leg, trying to comfort her.

"She doesn't let men see her the way she really is. I'm sure he didn't know," I said.

She looked at me. "Thanks, Onalee." She wiped her eyes and blew her nose. "Anyway, since you were trying to figure this thing out, I thought I'd better tell you about this. I don't know if it means anything."

"I'm glad you did. I don't know either. Except, it reinforces my opinion of Linda Lorian. She is a nasty one."

"Have you talked to her?"

"Yes, thanks to your tip about being able to find her at the tennis club. But, I didn't really get anywhere with her."

"And you know about Mike being a hunter?" she asked.

"I did hear that. Actually, Linda is, too."

"Oh, really? Then it must have been her, that witch," Janet muttered and started down the trail. Lucas, still concerned, stayed right by her side. Julian and I followed them, in silence. After another few minutes, she turned around and said, "I just hope she doesn't get away with it."

"Me too. But I don't think the police are trying too hard to nab her. Of course, maybe she didn't do it."

Janet, turned on her heel to face me, "Do you really believe that?"

"No. I think it probably was her. But how can we prove it?"

"I don't know." We walked and talked and by the time we had completed the circuit, our plan was in place. We would take turns tailing our quarry until she made a fatal false move. As they always do. Then we would pounce on the evil Linda P. and see that she was prosecuted to the full extent of the law.

Janet volunteered for the first shift, so I said I'd go home and stock us up on stakeout sustenance. It turned out that Janet was also a fan of sugar and spice, so I planned to make a curried cereal snack and my famous World's Best Peanut Butter cookies.

* * * * *

191

After returning home, I worked on the appraisal for a few more hours and wound it up, eighty-nine pages, three rent comparables and four sale comparables. I would take it to the post office for delivery in the morning. Then I stopped over to see Mrs. Stirnaman.

She was back in her room after the surgery and was sleepy but coherent. The procedure had gone well and she now sported a brand new hip. She was happy to hear that Julian was staying with me. According to the nurses, she'd be in the hospital for a few more days and then would need to go to a rehab facility for a couple of weeks.

Mrs. S. dropped back off to sleep in mid-sentence and I tiptoed out. I sped home. It was time to cook. It seemed like forever since I'd spent any time in my kitchen.

After a quick check, I found that I had all of the necessary ingredients for my creations. I felt like an artist with a box full of paints, as I pulled down my favorite sky blue colored mixing bowl from the cupboard. It is just the right size for my biggest batches of cookies. As I mixed and measured, and measured and mixed, I began to feel at peace with the world, something I realized I hadn't felt for days.

I worked away for an hour or so, resulting in a cookie jar full of cookies and three large zip-lock bags of zesty snacks. I washed

the dishes, then delivered a care package to
Janet, stationed outside the P.-Lorian house.

*****

The following morning the alarm sounded 'neath
a still darkened sky. As I lay there, I heard
distant rumblings of thunder and the soft
patter of rain. My eyelids fell shut and I
drifted off again. About twenty minutes later
I awoke and jumped out of bed before I could
be lulled back to sleep. The thunderheads had
already moved on to the east, but rain,
glorious rain, was still streaming down the
window.

I pulled on my jogging shorts and tee
shirt, tied up my running shoes, grabbed the
J-Dog and scrambled out the door. The rain was
steady, but in the warm, humid air, the cool
water was welcome, as we splashed our way down
the street to the bike path. I decided, as a
change of pace, to run through the camping
areas of the park. All of the campers seemed
to be sleeping in, cozy within their tents and
RV's.

I ran down through the two campgrounds and
on to the main beach road. The heavy air was
laden with the scent of cedar. A group of
birds were hanging out, smiles curved across
their beaks as they enjoyed the feeling of
cool rain washing through their feathers. The
long, dusty dry spell was finally broken.

193

At the main road we turned to the left and jogged down to the beach. This morning, the lake was burnished pewter and completely still. I trotted on the hard sand at the water's edge while Julian zig zagged between me and the dunes. Eventually, we wound our way home.

After my shower, coffee and two graham crackers, I took my reports in to the post office. With a long walk and breakfast under his belt, Julian would be fine by himself for a while. Janet and I had agreed that we would tail Linda P. until she appeared to be settled in for the night and would then resume our vigil early the next morning. Normally we would each be responsible for every other day. But Janet had agreed to start yesterday and stay on the case until my report was delivered. Then it would be my turn.

At about 8:45, I called Janet's cell phone for her location then drove to parley with her. My car was now outfitted as a rolling treasure trove of junk food. At the last minute I'd grabbed a small jar of extra-fiery curry powder and tucked that into my shorts pocket, just in case. Also, I'd brought along my mystery book. I couldn't do much on my next appraisal, so it appeared that I was forced to take the day off.

Janet had parked on a side street off the highway, near Northern Michigan's poshest gym.

Hot Property

I pulled in behind Janet and slipped into the passenger seat of her car. She proceeded to give me her report on the activities of Linda P., both yesterday and early this morning. It didn't sound as if Linda had been very productive. Her time had been spent more or less, flitting about to various shops, when she hadn't been lolling around her house. Janet finished by stating that no irregularities had been spotted since she'd been on stake-out. Currently, Linda P. was in the gym, apparently working out, and she'd been there roughly thirty minutes, according to Janet's log.

Janet left and I flopped back into my car seat. Slouching down, I watched the front door of the gym for what seemed to be a very long time. I checked my watch. It had been four minutes since Janet's departure and was now 9:10. It was early, yet. Too early for lunch, and I'd had breakfast. The sun had broken through the clouds and now shone directly on the container of cookies. I could almost smell them, I thought with a chuckle. Wait a minute, me thinks I can smell them. There is an unmistakable undercurrent of peanut butter in the air.

I carefully pried one edge of the container up just a tinge to see if that was indeed what I smelled. Peanut buttery air escaped in a whoosh, as I glimpsed a cookie nestled in its bed of tin foil. Uh oh, the top cookie was damaged slightly. A crack had broken off one small piece. It was no longer tidy, but it would be easy to remove that piece and neaten things back up. I gently reached in for it and laid it on my tongue. The tiny taste said it all. Yes, I truly had accomplished the perfect batch. The morsel fell apart in my mouth, I swallowed, and it was gone. Carefully, placing the top back on the container, I resumed my watch.

Thinking it over, I concluded that it had been a good idea to allow myself that small bite of cookie. I could now devote my entire attention to watching for Linda, rather than having part of my mind taken up with thoughts of peanut butter.

Many minutes more dragged by, although people did enter and leave on occasion. And here comes our Linda P. She must have showered and put her street clothes back on. Her car was about a half block away, and I watched as she strode over to it, jumped in and roared off. I had to scramble to get my car started and take off after her. Luckily, there weren't very many other cars on the road just then and I could easily keep her in sight.

At the highway, Linda turned and drove towards Petoskey. I slipped in behind her at an unobtrusive distance, and we proceeded a few miles to a gourmet foods and meat market. Linda found a parking space near the front door and sauntered up to the store. If she is buying food, I reasoned, she will probably be heading home. So I parked on the side of the lot closest to Petoskey, with the Honda's nose pointing out in takeoff position.

Shoppers came and went and once again, our Linda emerged, this time with a sack of groceries. She peeled out, with me faithfully tagging along far behind her. She made two more stops before driving home. I allowed myself a small atta-girl moment. I'd never tailed anyone before but I seemed to be doing a great job of keeping the perp in sight without arousing her suspicions.

Linda stayed at her house for a very long hour and a half, then zipped off to Rudolph's Place, one of our most exclusive restaurants. My, my, my. Didn't money just flow through that woman's fingers.

I was getting hungry myself. The bite of cookie, along with the rest of it and one other, hadn't filled me up. I had a coffee yogurt on ice and intended to supplement that with a few handfuls of curried snacks, and then a couple of cookies. An hour went by and then another one.

This private eye stuff is for the birds. Not only was I really bored, but I was finding that it wasn't such a great idea to pack so many cookies. The Jaws of Life might have to be used to cut me out of this car by the end of my shift.

Finally, Linda P emerged with several other women also dressed in designer-casual attire. They hugged one another stiffly and went to their cars. Linda and I then drove to the R & L office in our respective vehicles. She parked right up front in one of the spaces the staff tries to keep open for customers, while I parked across the street and down a ways.

As she disappeared through the door, I reached over to my nearly empty cookie container. By now, I was munching along on cookie number ten or eleven, and it tasted just as succulent as the first one had. I popped the rest of it in my mouth. The sun was really beating in and I closed my eyes against the glare. I must also confess that I seemed to be in a bit of a sugary haze.

I might have dropped off, because I seemed to be walking down the beach with Rick Sommers. We were laughing and talking, just like old times, when all of a sudden someone yanked open my car door.

Chapter Twenty-four

I looked up into the ferocious eyes of Linda P. as she screamed, "What are you doing here? You've been following me all day."

Things were happening too fast for me. A siren wailed and people streamed out of the R & L office building as a back-drop to Linda's unending tirade.

She leaned in even closer. "Stay away from me. Do you hear me? I have had it with you. You're crazy."

Spittle, like shrapnel slammed into my cheek. Who is the crazy one, here?

The siren ended as a car careened to a stop within several feet of the Honda. Linda was still screeching, seemingly unaware of the cops. She was reaching for me, and I think she planned to drag me out of the car, possibly scalp first, when someone came between us.

"We'll take over from here, Mrs. Lorian. Let's settle down a bit and you can tell me what's going on."

The voice had become very familiar to me over the past several weeks. I looked up.

"Hello, Ms. O'Conner. Fancy meeting you here. I want you to stay right there while I talk with Mrs. Lorian."

They walked away. I noticed Mike Lorian, Marissa, my buddy Henry Greeley and some other people I didn't know, standing at a safe distance. Their heads all seemed to be on swivels, looking first at me, then at Linda and Costas. Marissa and Henry exchanged a few words and then came over to me.

"What was that all about?" Henry asked.

"Heck if I know. I had just pulled off here for a couple of minutes to eat my lunch, when Linda came at me like a komodo dragon with seven shots of espresso in his belly."

"Why would you stop here to eat your lunch?" Marissa's question sounded tinged with suspicion.

Their attention was diverted by Costas striding back towards us.

"Mind if I have a few moments alone with Ms. O'Conner?" he asked, and they backed off.

"Mrs. Lorian tells me you've been following her all day. She wants me to arrest you, or, at the very least place a restraining order on you." He poked his head inside my car and sniffed several times. "What is that smell? Curry. No, there's something else. . . . Just a hint of . . . peanut butter?"

200

"I just had lunch."

He stood back and crossed his arms. "And have you been tailing Mrs. Lorian?"

"Of course not. How preposterous. If she had to work for a living like I do, she'd realize that I don't have time for such shenanigans."

"Okay, then how do you explain the fact that you just happen to be parked within sight of the R & L offices?"

"I had just finished lunch and was in the process of reviewing comparable data. Much of my work is accomplished by visual inspections, Detective. I don't just sit at my computer all day."

"Tell me, just to help me better understand your 'work'. Do appraisers always snore as they ponder their data?"

"I wasn't snoring."

"According to Linda Lorian, she could hear you from clear across the street. If you charge by the hour for your appraisals, you'd better consider giving your customers a rebate."

"We don't charge by the--"

Interrupting me, he said, "Actually, I could care less how you charge for your services. Anyway, what will it be, Hardy Girl, will you cease and desist, in your harassment of Mrs. Lorian, or should we file a restraining order?"

"You know she probably did it, don't you?"

"Did what?"

"Killed Jonathon Richmond and Amber Czinski."

"She might have, along with about a dozen other people. Not to mention my favorite suspect, Onalee O'Conner."

"Come on. I'll bet if you search the Lorian's house, you'll find the murder weapon. . . Camille," I'm afraid my smirk wasn't becoming, but I was under a lot of stress just then.

He glowered. "I'll keep that in mind. And for your information, Camille is a guy's name in France. If you were at all cultured you would have heard of Camille Pissarro, the Impressionist painter, or Camille Saint Sans, the composer. Now, will you leave Mrs. Lorian alone or do I have to haul you in?"

"Actually, her name is Linda Pendleton-Lorian. Why don't you call her that?"

"Don't push your luck," he growled.

"All right, yes. I'll leave her alone." I peered up at him. "You don't like hyphenators, either, do you?"

His eyebrows shot up and I think his lips might have twitched a tad. "No. Does anybody?" He turned on his heel and strode back to his car.

Chapter Twenty-five

I started the CRV and cruised away. Marissa, appearing even more statuesque than usual beside the squat figure of Henry Greely, was framed in my rear view mirror as I turned the corner. Marissa and Rob Darnell would have made such a good looking couple. And he was truly a great guy. With the shortage of good men in Northern Michigan, and quite possibly, the entire free world, why had she dumped him?

I called it a day. My appraisal was out the door. It was sunny and warm. Summer was flitting by and I had not spent much time sun bathing and swimming. I needed to rectify that. After all, it was half my pay.

At home, I served Julian his lunch and then took him on his rounds. Afterwards, I quickly changed into my favorite swimsuit, one of the tankini styles that have the tactical advantages of a two-piece while obscuring a certain amount of indulgence in peanut butter cookies. I grabbed my beach bag, always packed and ready to go, my book and a legal pad along with several pencils.

The beach was lively for mid-week. A group of teen-agers were playing volleyball near the concession stand. Colorful beach umbrellas dotted the sand and lots of swimmers were splashing about in the water. A gentle breeze buffeted me as I laid out my faded beach blanket. It had been dead still in town, which had, unfortunately resulted in my slightly drowsy condition at the stake-out. The wind kicked up the waves a bit and created a small surf. As I lay down, I could hear my favorite background noise, children laughing and yelling, as waves crashed against the shore.

I took out my legal pad and pencil. Just as Marti had done several weeks ago, I wrote down all of the suspects' names. Then I would go back through and write what I now knew about each of them. Linda P.-Lorian was still at the very top of my list. She had a motive, jealousy. She knew how to shoot a gun and she probably had access, at least to Jonathon. I wasn't sure, though, that Amber would have let her into her condo. Then again, maybe the door had been unlocked. It had been the middle of the day, when I'd found the body, so Linda P. or whoever may have just walked in.

If I ignored my personal dislike of the woman, I had to admit that she probably didn't rank above her husband, Mike Lorian, and possibly still Janet Richmond as suspects. Mike also had jealousy as a motive, and he also could shoot. And he had that twitching eye. I didn't know about Janet's ability with weaponry. And since she was now kind of my crime-solving partner, I didn't like to see her name on the list at all, let alone tied for first place. I added Marti's new squeeze, Frank Ryan, to the list, but I couldn't see what connection he had to Amber.

All this time and I hadn't gotten very far with my sleuthful endeavors. Although, come to think of it, our original list had had three additional names. Roger Bandsinger, the township zoning official was eliminated because of his alibi. Marti had included me on the original list but I was, heretofore, removing myself. Finally, I could also eliminate Amber, because someone else already had.

Unless I found a connection between Amber and Frank Ryan, it appeared that I should focus on Jonathon's torrid personal life rather than his real estate developing. That should please Marti. I started another list of questions I needed answered.

Does Janet Richmond know how to handle a gun?

Was Janet telling the truth about the argument between Linda P.-Lorian and Mike, her husband?

If so, who were they arguing about?

Did Mike know about Jonathon's affair with his wife, Linda P.?

Hot Property

If I could prove that it was Linda P., would they lock her up and throw away the key?

Will Rick Sommers ever call me again?

Is Camille really a guy's name in France?

I laid down my pencil and rolled over. What was nagging at the back of my mind? Someone had lied to me, but I couldn't quite put two and two together. The sun, now that I was facing directly into it, was scorching. That's enough. Time to go for a swim.

The water was turquoise today. An artist friend of mine once asked me why Little Traverse Bay changed to so many different colors. Who can say? But now that I've seen a lot of oceans and other lakes, around the world, I realize that our ever changing lake is truly magical.

The water was cool but actually warmer than usual for late June. It is rare that anybody, at least anyone sober and over the age of ten, plunges into these waters before July.

I swam for about twenty minutes then rolled over on my back to gaze at the hills hugging the shore. Despite the heat of the day, I was starting to get chilled. It was time to leave this crystal water world and warm up in the sun.

I stayed at the beach for a couple of hours. After all, the experts now say that we aren't getting enough Vitamin D. All too soon, the time came to pack up my blanket and mosey on home. I smiled as the thought struck me that in two days' time, Rosie and her entourage would be in Petoskey.

I still hadn't heard whether I knew any of the other attendants in the wedding party. The world of competitive badminton is a rather small one, and there was a good chance I'd know a few of the other brides maids. Every time Rosie and I had talked, she was vague on the details. All I knew for sure was that everyone was coming to northern Michigan.

* * * * *

The following day I straightened up the house, paid bills and did other household chores. Julian and I romped around the county park, ate our meals together and relaxed on my deck. All the while, I mulled over the list of suspects and unanswered questions. Eventually, it occurred to me that there was another connection I hadn't mined to the fullest. I called R and L. Henry wasn't in but I was told to try his cell phone.

"Hi Henry," I said as he came on the line. "Onalee, here. How's life in the fast lane?"

"Hello, love. Peachy as always." I could hear the smile in his voice.

"What are you up to?"

"I'm in Office-World doing techy things."

I laughed. "How about a gelato at Lulu's?" I asked, knowing he couldn't resist.

"Oh, you are the naughty temptress. Who told you I started a strict diet this morning?"

"Then iced tea at McDonald's it is."

"Hold your horses, Onalee. Have you tried Lulu's latest creation? Passion fruit tiramisu. It's to die for. I'll meet you there in ten minutes."

Chapter Twenty-six

I drove in to town and parked my car near Lulu's. Henry was already there and sitting at a small table outside the cafe. We went inside and both decided on double dips. I went with the passion fruit tiramisu and added a scoop of salted caramel. Henry decided on tart cherry for his second choice. I paid for both of our cones with a twenty. The kid behind the counter took my money, gave me change and with a big smile, said "Thank you, Ma'am."

I frowned, trying to figure out the exact moment when I had slid into the objectionable state of Ma'am hood. Henry watching me, chuckled.

"You'll forever be the youthful Miss or Ms. Onalee O'Conner, to me, Love."

"Thanks, Henry."

We strolled back outside and sat in our chairs. "I see you've recovered from yesterday's debacle," Henry said. He leaned in over the table. "Tell me, cupcake, was it true that you were stalking our Linda Lorian?"

I'd taken a dainty bite of the gelato. "Ummm, Henry, you're right about this passion fruit." Its cool smoothness caressed my tongue.

He grinned. "It's beyond superb. Now, don't weasel out on me."

"Do you think she killed Jonathon?"

He chuckled. "That's why you were tailing her? Did you catch her in any criminal activity other than spending more of Michael's money in one day than most third world countries spend on their education systems in a year?"

I licked up a spoonful of salted caramel and then eyed him. "We seem to be avoiding each other's questions."

"Oh, girlfriend, I've missed you. Yes, yes, yes, Linda may have been the grim reaper, but let's just enjoy our treats without talk of all of that sadness."

"You're right," I said realizing then that the two deaths had hit him harder than he cared to admit. We savored our gelatos over small talk. Then got up and threw our small bowls away. At one point in the conversation, Henry and I had agreed to go clothes shopping. We ambled to a men's clothing store, several blocks away.

"I'm going out on a date on Saturday. I'm really in a dither about it. I've been out of that scene for so long," he said. Then he looked at me, a frown creasing his forehead. "You knew about David, right?"

"No. What happened?"

"He left. He couldn't live without his kids."

We'd stopped and I hugged him. "I'm so sorry, Henry."

"Thanks, Onalee," he said as he clung to me. Then he wiped the back of his hand across his eyes. "Sorry about that. It's been three months but it gets to me sometimes, when I least expect it. I still love him but I know I've got to move on." He stepped out of my embrace and managed a small smile. "You know, it really is true that it's better to have had great love, if even for a few years, than to have never experienced that. I'll always be glad I had him in my life."

I guess I looked a little wistful because Henry squeezed my arm and said, "It'll happen for you, too, Onalee. The right guy is out there." He stepped back and studied me. "That reminds me, what's happening with Rick Sommers? Marissa told me," he added.

I shook my head. "I'm afraid that was over before it started. Anyway, let's find you some gay apparel."

He groaned. "You're so droll." We entered the store. "I'm glad you're with me. I need help."

"What do you mean, Henry? You always look natty."

"Thanks to David. He picked out all of my clothes."

"Don't you gay guys all know about this stuff?" I said then looked up into scornful eyes.

"Onalee, don't tell me you buy into that stereotype. Shame on you."

Oops. "So, next you're going to tell me you don't like the opera?"

"No, I adore the opera. Now let's get busy." He walked over to a rack of jackets. "I want something that quietly asserts, 'Baltimore Oriole' not shouts 'peacock'."

"Gotcha." I said but I needed more information. "Where are you going to wear it?"

"We're going on a dinner cruise. You know how it gets chilly up here on the water and especially at night."

I helped him rifle through the rack. He pulled out a couple of coats that I nixed. He truly was fashion blind. Then we found a soft, buttery yellow leather one. "Ooh, try that one."

He pulled it on, zipped it up and then turned to show me his front, side and rear silhouettes. "What do you think?"

"I like it but it's a little snug."

He tried a larger one.

Again I inspected him in three D. "Perfect."

He gazed at himself in the mirror. "It's slimming, don't you think?"

"Yes, indeedy. You look like a million bucks in that, Henry."

He grinned. "I'll take it."

We were walking back towards our cars when Henry turned to me. "Thank you, Onalee, for sharing your clothes sense. I know you wanted to talk about the murders, so go ahead and ask me questions and I'll tell you everything I know."

Chapter Twenty-seven

"Have you got any idea who did it?"

He shook his head. I've thought a lot about it, because it's sort of scary. Two people in our small office. Murdered. Will there be more? And, I liked Jonathon. He was a good guy. He came off as pretty macho. You know, a man's man? But he never felt threatened by my gayness. Actually, everyone in the office is cool about that. To answer your question, I just don't have any ideas. What have you come up with?"

"Did you know about all of his affairs?"

"I heard things. But you've got to understand, I'm not tuned into hetero d'amour. I didn't even know about Jonathon and Amber until Marissa clued me in. Though I guess I should have figured it out. She wasn't much of a secretary. Of course, I know that we of the technologically challenged generation can be a bit high maintenance for the younger crowd."

"You two didn't get along?"

"Not really."

"Was she homophobic?"

He laughed. "More like ludite-aphobic. She'd get so irritated by my lack of computer prowess. She was forever having to help me download my listing pictures, and I can't give her any kudos for patience."

That didn't surprise me. Amber had struck me as an extremely self-centered person. "Do you think, now that Amber is also dead, that we can assume that Jonathon was killed because of his sashaying around with multiple women rather his real estate developing?"

He nodded his head. "Yes, I always thought it was a crime of the heart. Didn't you?"

"I do now. What do you know about Linda P.-Lorian?"

Chuckling, he said, "Probably not as much as you do at this point, Stake-out Girl. To tell you the truth, I've always tried to avoid Her Queenliness. Not that it was hard to do. We office peons were not in her class, doncha know," he said with a turned down mouth and nose lifted in the air.

"You knew about her and-"

"Jonathon?" He frowned, "Oh yes. It was very hush-hush and it was also all anyone could talk about for a very, very long time."

"What did people say?"

"We were all appalled, as you can imagine. I think everyone likes Michael and it was such a skanky thing to do."

"Do you think he knew?"

"I think he had to have."

"Could it have tipped Michael over the edge?"

"Is that your theory?"

"It's one of them, but of course Linda P. and possibly Jonathon's wife, Janet also have motives."

He turned towards me, and I'd have to describe his grin as a bit feral. "All I can say is, we've got to hope and pray it was the Lovely Linda."

"You like Janet?" We were back at my car now and I stood by the door.

"Oh, yeah. She's a sweetie. And Michael is a great guy. A real straight shooter," he said but I noticed a slight frown and he looked away.

"His twitching eye?"

He swung back towards me. "Yes. He has been acting very nervous lately."

"Do you know what he was doing at the time Jon was killed?"

"The police talked to all of us. Ooh la la, but they have some lookers on the force, especially that detective."

I looked at him incredulously, "You don't mean Camille Costas, do you?"

He grinned. "Bingo. Camille, eh? He must be named after Camille Pissaro, the French Impressionist painter. Anyway, he is hopelessly hetero, I'm afraid." He sighed.

"Anyway, you were saying?"

"Oh, yeah. Of course, I remember a lot of details about that day because of going back over everything for the Luscious Camille. As I told him, I had showings that afternoon so I was in and out of the office. Michael and I talked because one of the cottages my people were interested in was his listing. That was about 2:00. We made it brief because he had to leave."

I leaned against my car. "Where was he going, do you remember?"

"Yes. He had a listing appointment." He leaned in, "He's a real rainmaker. Everyone thought that Jon was the brains behind R & L, but I always thought it was more Michael."

"Do you know what property he listed?"

He eyed me. "I'm not going to regret telling you this, am I, Baby Cakes?"

"No, no."

He sighed. "You did put up with me at Helberstutz Men's Wear and because of you I now own this fine jacket," he said holding up the blue and tan striped Helberstutz bag.

"Yes, I did."

"All right, it's the Randall cottage on Crooked Lake. But Onalee, what are you planning to do?"

"Probably nothing, but thanks Henry. Have fun on your date." I said as I opened my car door.

"Not so fast, Missy. Don't go doing something silly that gets us both in hot water. Promise?" He held my door open as I tried to pull it closed.

"I promise, you big bully." He smiled then and shut the door. I fired up the Honda and sped out of town. So, I'd gotten at least one of my questions answered. Camille actually is a guys' name in France.

Chapter Twenty-eight

Back at my house I was greeted by a tail wagging Julian holding one of his stuffed animals in his mouth. How cute. "Hey sweet dog," I said, rubbing behind his ears. "Wanna go for a walk?" His tail beat the air even harder and he yipped. "Okay, but drop Mr. Froggie. . . . Drop your toy or we won't go out."

We'd been through this before. The first time he'd wanted to take one of his animals outside I let him. About a half block into our walk, he realized he couldn't hang onto his toy and chase squirrels. The upshot was that I traipsed around the neighborhood carrying a slobbery stuffed yellow chicken. But this time, by my stern tone, Julian knew I meant business, dropped the frog and out the door we went for a quiet walk.

When we returned, I hopped on the computer and looked up Mike Lorian's listings on Crooked Lake. He only had one and the owners' name was Randall. I jotted down the address, changed into my bankerly attire and zipped out the door. It was 3:30, and there was still plenty of time for sleuthing. On the drive over I thought about Mike Lorian. He had a strong motive to shoot Jonathon but what about Amber? The only reason I could think of that he'd murder her was that she had figured out he was the killer.

The Randall property was on the back side of Crooked Lake, down a gravel lane off the main road. The house was situated in a grove of trees and built very close to the lake, much closer than a structure could be built under current laws. It was a classic cottage with light blue board and batten siding. A red and black, diamond-shaped R and L sign was in the yard. As I turned into the short drive I saw a slender, elderly woman working in her flower garden. She stood up as I got out of my car.

With a gloved hand she shielded her eyes from the sun's glare. "Hello. Can I help you?"

"Are you Mrs. Randall?" I said, holding a clip board and pen.

"Yes, I am," she said and smiled.

"Hi, I'm Lee O'Donnell, and I'm from R and L, just doing an internal audit on all of our listings." I gave her an engaging grin. "I'm sure you're busy but can I ask you a few questions? It won't take more than a few minutes."

"Certainly. Do you need to see the house?"

"No. I just need to verify the information submitted to the Multiple Listing Service. Let's see. Was the house listed on June Fourth?"

She thought for a minute. "That sounds about right. I have the paper work inside. Come on in."

She held open the door, and we entered her living room. The walls were covered in knotty pine with a large picture window on the opposite wall. "Wow. The lake is right there."

She smiled at my reaction. "Yes, I sit here with my morning coffee and watch families of ducks swim right by me." Walking over to an old roll top desk, she pulled out the listing agreement and examined it for a few minutes. "Yes, it's dated the Fourth." She looked up, "Please have a seat," she said and sat in the desk chair as I sank into a comfortable couch.

"Michael Lorian was the listing agent?"

She nodded. "Yes. Some friends of mine recommended him."

I pretended to read another question off the clip board. "Do you happen to remember what time Mr. Lorian came out to list your house?"

"Uh huh. We had a 2:30 appointment and he was prompt."

"Excellent. That's what we want to hear about our agents." I scribbled some notes on my clip board.

"And did Mr. Lorian proceed to take pictures and measurements of your home?"

"Yes, he did. I thought he was very thorough."

"Do you remember about how long he was here?"

"It was close to four o'clock by the time he was finished. I know because as soon as he left, I started to cook dinner. I was getting peckish," she said and smiled.

Uh oh, it was getting close to her dinner time again. Besides, I got my answer. Mike Lorian was here at the time of Jonathon's death. It was time to wrap this up. "On the whole, would you say you're satisfied with Mr. Lorian and R and L at this time?"

"Absolutely, and I appreciate your keeping tabs on everything."

Smiling, I got to my feet and shook hands with her. "Thank you so much for your time, Mrs. Randall."

On the drive back to town, I took stock. I could cross another suspect off my list, twitching eye and all. That still left Linda P., Janet Richmond and possibly Marti's Frank.

I hadn't talked with Janet since the dismal ending to our stake-out. She'd called but I hadn't had time to get back to her. Could she be the killer? Did she know how to shoot a gun? She couldn't be a murderess, could she?

I decided to swing by her house on my way home. First I pulled off the road and called Marti. I told her if I hadn't called her back within twenty minutes, to call the cops and send them to Janet's house. She was only too happy to hear that I was back in crime-solving mode and said she would set her alarm for 4:30.

"Why would you set your alarm?"

"So I don't forget."

I did not care for her tone of voice with an unstated but understood "Duh." Here I was, putting my life on the line to possibly clear her Boy Toy, and she didn't have the decency to sit on the edge of her seat, rigid with fear for my safety.

"Alrighty then," I chirped. "I hope I'm not putting you out." I said and maneuvered back onto the street.

The Richmond house was located in a woodsy area close to the community college. Even though it was only ten or fifteen years old, it featured craftsman-style architectural details including a large veranda with an overhanging roof. For all of Jonathon's wealth, it wasn't imposing, just classy. I wondered if that was Janet's influence. I parked in the drive and hustled up to the door. After I rang the bell, I heard Lucas bark and soon Janet threw open the door.

"Onalee. What a nice surprise," she said. "I heard what happened with Linda P," she chuckled. "I thanked my lucky stars it wasn't me that got caught. That would have really been embarrassing."

"Yes, it was quite the mare's nest."

She laughed again. "How horrible for you."

I was getting slightly irritated with all of my crime-solving partners today. "I'm just happy that you were spared," I said sounding a tad unconvincing.

She sobered up and opened the door. "Come in come in. I loved all of the snacks you made, by the way." Lucas ran up to me and I leaned down to pet him. We were in the living room and I surveyed all of the walls.

"No wild animal heads?"

"Not on your life. The Lorians can have our . . . my share. Come on back to the porch. Want some iced tea or water?"

"Water would be great," I said, intending to watch her around any food or beverage that I'd ingest. The kitchen was on our way and she stopped and filled my glass with water and

225

ice, then led me out to a narrow room off the rear of the house. Screened windows all along the back wall overlooked a wooded ravine. "It's like we're in a tree house," I said.

She smiled, "It's my favorite room in the house."

Opposite the windows was an oversized couch and a long, low coffee table. I sat on the couch and placed my water on the table.

As I turned towards Janet, she asked, "What's on your mind, Onalee?

I told her about going to the Randall cottage and Michael Lorian's alibi.

"I'm glad it wasn't him. But who does that leave?"

"There might be someone we haven't thought of, yet. But, otherwise, the list is getting kind of short."

"There's the tree-hugger guy."

"Yes, Frank."

"And, Linda P.-" her voice trailed off and she looked down, frowning. "Is that the reason for your tête-à-tête today?"

I studied her as I spoke, "I didn't have any motive to kill your husband and I don't think Frank had any connection to Amber." I paused. "Linda P had a motive to seek revenge on both of them—" It was my turn to trail off.

Janet was still looking at the floor. "I suppose I had the same motive as Linda and also opportunity." She looked into my eyes. "I already told you that I was with Lucas at the time of Jon's death and, actually, when Amber was murdered as well. I've always been a bit of a loner."

"Did you do it?" I asked, softly.

She'd been looking down again but she raised her eyes to mine and said, "No."

It sounded convincing, but I'm pretty sure I don't always know when someone is lying to me. "Do you know how to shoot a gun?"

She gave me a rueful smile. "You know nothing about me, Onalee. I grew up on a farm over by Onaway. We didn't have a lot of money, but my dad hunted and fished and we grew a lot of what we ate. The five of us kids were expected to do our part, and we all did. Plus we were supposed to do our best in school and make something of ourselves.

"I was fishing almost as soon as I could walk and had learned to shoot a gun by the time I'd traded my Barbie dolls for boys. So, I won't blame you if you keep me on your list."

Wow, and here I'd had her pegged as from a wealthy socialite family. We talked a bit longer but it was awkward, and I left after a few more minutes. As I was driving away I remembered to report in to Marti.

Chapter Twenty-nine

During the evening, the calm waters of Little
Traverse Bay lured me in with my kayak. It was
a very still evening and only one other boat,
a mid-sized sailboat, and I were out. My
bright yellow paddle sliced through the azure
seas as I skimmed along towards Petoskey's
waterfront park. I had a feeling that the next
several days with all of the wedding hoopla
would be a maelstrom of activity, and I soaked
in the peace radiating from the lake. An hour
or so later, I in my boat, had a perfect seat
in which to watch the sunset, though the green
flash remained elusive.

* * * * *

Mrs. Stirnaman was graduating to rehab today,
and Julian and I were in my car, on our way to
visit her. I'd called ahead to check on her
therapy schedule so that we could arrive on
her break time. Permission for Julian to come
along had been granted by the nursing staff.
The rehab was a separate wing of Emmet County
Hospital. We found her room easily, and there
she was, sitting in a chair beside her bed,
reading.

"Julian, my dear baby dog! I have missed you so much." She held her arms open and Julian, tail sweeping the air, bounded over to her. He licked her and licked her and licked her and then leaped into the small space between her bed and nightstand and pirouetted.

Mrs. Stirnaman threw back her head and laughed. "That's his happy dance," she said looking at me with shining eyes. "What a wonderful surprise." Julian bounded back to her side, and sat, gazing up at her.

"I thought a reunion might spice up everyone's day," I said, grinning.

"Has he been eating well?"

"Oh, yes and he gets plenty of exercise."

"Wonderful. I can't thank you enough, Onalee." She paused then said, hesitantly, "Can I ask something of a rather . . . delicate nature?"

I'd glanced out the window but at that my head swiveled back to Mrs. Stirnaman. "Sure."

"How have Julian's stools, been. Are they firm?"

I laughed. "Yes, they've been everything you could hope for in a stool."

"Hello, Doctor Parks."

Hot Property

I turned towards the door and saw a handsome man grinning at Mrs. Stirnaman. How much of that potty discussion had he heard?

"How are you feeling today, Mrs. S? Hey, boy." He dropped to his haunches and held out his hand for Julian to sniff him.

"I'm doing great. You must be a dog person, Doctor," Mrs. Stirnaman said. "And I'd like to introduce you to my lovely neighbor, Miss Onalee O'Conner. She's taking great care of Julian for me."

We said our hellos.

"Doctor, Onalee is a runner too. That is, when she can find the time. She owns her own business. And you should taste her pies—"

Ahghghg. My cheeks were on fire. "Wow. That's a big boat out there." I cut in before she had a chance to go on. There was an expansive view of the bay from the window.

I saw Mrs. Stirnaman glower at me but the apparently eligible physician stepped closer to the window. "I'll say," he said, flashing me a smile. "It's a great day to be on the lake." Then he turned back to Mrs. Stirnaman and said, "Keep up the great work in rehab. I'll check in on you next week. Nice to meet you Miss O'Conner."

He left and Mrs. Stirnaman rounded on me. "Onalee, he's a doctor and you saw for yourself how nice he is, not to mention good looking. Now, I'll find out the exact day and time next week when he'll be back. You need to put some lipstick on and hop on back here. Some rouge wouldn't hurt either. Don't let him get away."

"He's probably married."

"Did you see a ring?"

"I didn't look."

She shook her head and sighed. "Well, I did and there wasn't one."

"That still doesn't necessarily, mean that he's single."

Her roguish grin appeared. "Onalee, at my age, I can get away with saying what's on my mind, even if it's a bit outlandish. People think I'm precious, so I came right out and asked him. He is one hundred percent unspoken for."

"He's a lot younger than I am." I said, putting my hand on her shoulder. "I appreciate your help but I think we'd better leave the poor man alone."

"Oh, pshaw. You're getting a little long in the tooth, Onalee, if you don't mind my saying so. I don't think you can afford to be so fussy," she said, continuing to "speak her mind."

Hot Property

We talked a while longer, Mrs. Stirnaman
gave Julian a last hug and then Mr. J. and I
skedaddled home.

*****

Just to be festive, Julian and I took our
lunch on the back deck. I had one more, free
afternoon before Rosie would be here. I had to
get the goods on Linda P. I'd asked Janet who
Linda's friends were, but she said Ms. Lorian
ran in a high society circle, not the dog
walking group that Janet knew. My stake-out
had revealed some of her haunts, and I planned
to start at her health club.

I'd called before lunch and they had a
special introductory offer for people
interested in joining the club. It had been
awhile since I'd been to a gym. I hoped I'd
look stylish enough to fit in with the high
falooters of Northern Michigan. I threw my
running shorts and shirt in a work out bag and
hopped in the Honda bound for Northern
Latitude Fitness and Health Spa.

At the front desk a lithe twenty-something
signed me in, extricated one-hundred dollars
for my "bargain" introductory day pass. Then,
called into the inner sanctum for a guide to
accompany me on a tour of the building. The
facility was divided into two main areas, a
work-out portion and the spa. But, my one
hundred clam special was good only for the
work-out section. My guide, Trent, opened the

door to the spa, and we stepped into the reception area where all things serene greeted us. Water gurgled in a small fountain and the sound of a flute emanated softly from a hidden intercom system. The scent of lavender permeated the air.

Trent smiled and sotto voce, said, "Our motto is 'Let us pamper you.' There are facials and massages available here as well as all of the standard accoutrements such as a hot tub, sauna and steam bath. It is a truly luxurious way to spend a day."

I turned to him and said, "It sounds divine, and I'll keep that in mind for another day. But, as my dear friend, Linda says . . . you know Linda Pendleton Lorian, I'll bet," I shined a winning smile at Trent, "--those pounds you've packed on, Onalee, won't melt off in a hot tub. They need to be run to the ground on a treadmill."

Chuckling, Trent said, "That sounds exactly like her." He closed the door, and we walked into the fitness area. The noise level escalated as people ran and speed walked on tread mills and worked out on ellipses and stationary bicycles. Trent made a sweeping motion with his arms, "All of our equipment is state of the art."

I nodded. "It looks wonderful. Anyway, as I was saying, I'm here because of Linda. In fact, I thought she said she was going to be here today." I frowned slightly as I pretended to try recalling what she'd said.

He gave me a rueful smile. "I'm sorry. She was here, earlier. You missed her by about an hour."

Whew. That was good to know. I looked at my watch and plastered a chagrined look on my face. "Shoot. Do you know where she was headed? I might be able to catch up to her after my workout."

"No, I don't. But when we run into Zackary, her personal trainer, we can ask him if he knows. But, first, let me take you to the other gym where we hold our fitness classes."

How did I know that our Linda P. would have a personal trainer and that he'd be male? We looked in on a Yoga class and then Trent showed me the locker room and juice bar. He flashed a smile at me. "That's our facility. What do you think? Are you ready to make your commitment to fitness and join us for the next year?"

I smiled back, "I think I probably will. I know that Linda loves coming here and that makes it even more special. That reminds me, you were going to talk with Zackary?"

"That's right. Why don't you get your workout clothes on. Help yourself to a locker and any of the fitness machines you'd like to use. I'll round him up and send him over to talk with you if he's not with a client right now." He grinned again, "Enjoy your workout."

I whipped into the locker room, changed and hurried out to the gym. There I joined a line of glistening robots tramping on treadmills. I ran for about twenty minutes before eyeing a complete package on two legs as he strode up to me. He was tall, toned and in his twenties. Romance writers would describe his chiseled chin and direct manner as jolting their lovely young protagonists. As a somewhat beyond young heroine, I maintained my customary cool demeanor while deducting another forty points from my estimation of the forty-year old Linda P.

"Hi, Miss O'Conner? I'm Zachary. I was told you're trying to find Mrs. Lorian." Smiling brought out his dimples. Incredibly, that worked with the chiseled chin effect, I observed.

I slowed the treadmill's pace so that I could talk with the young steed. "Hi Zachary. I've heard so much about you. Linda says you're the greatest thing since sliced baguettes," I laughed.

He grinned. "She's great, isn't she?"

I wasn't a professional liar yet but I was becoming a stellar amateur prevaricator. "Yes, I love her to death." I said, hoping there hadn't been too much emphasis on the words "to death".

"Honestly, I, and I think, all of her friends are deeply worried about her since that terrible incident."

Slight frown lines creased his noble forehead. "Do you mean the murder of her husband's partner?"

"Yes. The poor thing took it really hard. You spend a lot of time with her. How do you think she's doing, Zachary? Really?"

"Um, okay I guess. She's a tough lady."

"Yeah, I know. Maybe I worry too much about her. But, I know that on top of everything else, the police were dogging her. I don't think she had much of an alibi, though why she'd be a suspect, I have no idea."

"I didn't know why, either."

I looked around, conspiratorially, then, leaning towards him a bit, lowered my voice. "We were all interviewed by the police about her."

Zachary looked away.

"I had heard that she was here and that people here vouched for her. If that's true, than that eases my mind."

He continued staring across the room. Finally, he turned back to me and gave me a hard look. "I think Mrs. L. may be at Seagrant's art studio. She mentioned she was going there this afternoon. You might still be able to catch her, if you hurry. After that, I believe she had some shopping to do at Mimi's." He turned abruptly and stalked away.

So much for that line of inquiry. I looked around the room. A lady on a nearby treadmill had slowed for her cool down phase. I wasn't positive but I thought she might have been with Linda P. outside the health club the other day. I slowed down as well. A few minutes later she stopped her machine and hopped off. I stopped mine, gave it a cursory drying off with my towel and fell into step behind her.

Her locker was down a bit from mine. We both cleaned up and began to get dressed. She was going to get away from me. I opened my purse wide and knocked it on the floor. Its clatter elicited a glance in my direction. Our eyes locked for an instant. "Oh, hi. Haven't I seen you with Linda Lorian?" I asked as I bent down and began scooping up my wallet, brush and related purse detritus.

She smiled. "Probably. We often work out at the same time but I had errands to run this morning."

"Yes, I know I've heard her mention you. I'm her friend Lee. I had hoped I might run into her today."

Hot Property

The woman frowned, slightly. "No, she rarely works out in the afternoons. I'm Gretchen, by the way," she said and loosened her hair from a scrunchy. She brushed it then eased over to the mirror and began applying make-up.

I strolled over and began running my comb through my hair. I wish I'd thought to pack that lipstick in my purse. Even if it was twenty-five years old, it still retained some of its color. I didn't know how long I could reasonably stand in front of the mirror with so few tools.

I shook my head. "I wasn't sure what her schedule was. She's been after me to come out here for forever and I just . . . I just wanted to do something that would make her happy." I searched Gretchen's vivid blue eyes, now outlined in smoky azure. Who could doubt my sincerity? I glanced around to make sure we weren't being overheard and lowered my voice. "She's been so upset lately."

Gretchen turned back to her reflection and applied some lipstick. "Yes, she has had a lot to deal with. Then on top of everything, some nut case was stalking her. Did she tell you about that?"

Ooh, I guess I didn't need any blusher today. "Um, yes, I heard something about that. But, I think it turned out that she was mistaken about that stalker. The main thing is, I just feel so bad that the police still have her as a person of interest. They've been terrible to her."

Gretchen arched one expertly shaped eye brow. "Really."

I nodded and pursed my lips. "Yes. I don't think she likes to talk about it. Does she even have an alibi? I know I wasn't with her when those murders occurred. I wish I had been so that I could've vouched for her." I put my comb away and brought out my brush.

She placed her lipstick in her purse, zipped it shut and turned to me. "I just hope they catch the guy who did it. I hardly feel safe in this town anymore. Nice meeting you, I've got to run." She hurried away before I could squeeze in another question or two.

I hadn't learned a lot for my one hundred dollar investment, but at least I now knew that Ms. Linda P. generally frequented this establishment in the morning. Ergo, she probably wouldn't have been here at the time of Jonathon's and Amber's deaths. I slid my brush into my purse, slung my workout bag over my shoulder and made my way out the door. Time was getting away from me and I wanted to pay a little visit to Linda's favorite art studio.

240

Chapter Thirty

On the drive over, I thought about my
activities. I was solidly in Henry's camp when
he said we should all "hope and pray" that our
Ms. Linda would turn out to be Linda Perp
Lorian. But, I wanted to be surer of it. If
she had an alibi, I wanted to know it. And, if
she didn't, all the merrier. In that case,
maybe we could send her, post haste, to the
big house.

Seagrant's was located outside of town on
the highway between Petoskey and Charlevoix.
As I pulled off the highway, I perused the
parking lot for the Linda P.-mobile. I didn't
see it, so I thought I was safe. I'd been in
this building a few times with friends who
were looking for unique gifts. It was divided
into an area with jewelry, knickknacks and
pottery, a gallery that displayed paintings
and other fine art mostly by local artists and
a working studio.

I stepped into the merchandise area. A few
people, mostly women, were milling around,
apparently spotting treasures that were
begging to be snapped up. A salesperson stood
behind a counter, chatting with a customer as

she processed her purchase. I made my way into the fine arts area of the building. There were a lot of paintings of local scenes. I sighed as I spotted the price tags. Some of them were gorgeous but they were destined to hang in homes other than my modest abode.

I walked through the gallery and into the studio. Here, natural light poured down from sky lights in the vaulted ceiling. A plump potato of a man, sitting in front of an easel looked up and smiled as I entered. "Hello. May I help you?" He seemed jolly.

I stepped over closer to see what he was working on. It was a painting of a cow approaching a hot air balloon that had landed in her pasture. "Wow, I love that."

He smiled at me. "They're such noble creatures, aren't they?" He dipped his brush and smeared some bluish grey into the sky.

"They sure are. Are you painting from your imagination or did you see that?"

"Funny you should ask. I did see it. Years ago in a farmer's field out east of town and I've always remembered it." With rapid strokes he brushed in a small stand of trees. "Only one cow in the herd was brave enough to go check out the balloon." He turned to me and grinned, "I always wondered what she'd tell her grand calves about that day."

"It may have changed her life."

"I'm almost certain that it did. Anyway, welcome to my studio. Are you an artist?" He was smiling at me again, deepening the crinkly areas around his eyes.

"Me? No, no. Though, it does look like fun."

"Oh, you can't beat it. You should give it a go. In fact, you can try it here."

"I think I've seen in the newspaper that you have classes."

He waved his hands in the universal signal of dismissal. "Ah, you don't need to pay for something you know nothing about. We charge $100.00 for the classes, but they are for people who want to perfect their craft. Each Tuesday evening, we get together and drink spirits and paint, draw or whatever you fancy and it's free. It's amazing how a shot or two will loosen you up. We call it our 'Paint the Town Red Tuesdays.' Tuesdays are such a blah night, don't you think? They're not horrid like Mondays but they lack the cache of hump night or the glory of the three weekend nights. So, we decided to give Tuesdays a raison d'etre." He examined the painting, added a cloud near the horizon then looked up at me again. "You should come. As I said, no charge, but you do need your own supplies. And wine."

"Sounds like fun," I surprised myself by saying. "I think I might try it. Should I call if I decide to come?"

He was talking with his hands again. "No, no, no. We're *tres* informal. Sometimes there are twenty of us and we're practically sitting in each other's laps. It's fun but we don't get as much work done." He laughed. "Other times, I've been the only one to show up."

This could be a horizon-expanding opportunity. On the other hand, it was getting late, and I needed to start my enquiries. I stole a glance at my watch, but, my new friend was not one to miss any details.

"I'm struck by the possibility that you didn't come here to be seduced into a life of dabbling in the fine arts and tippling fine wine. Is there something I can help you with?"

"Actually," I was finding it hard to lie to this fellow who reminded me of a twenty-first century Buddha, but I persevered. "I know my friend Linda Lorian comes here and I was hoping I could catch up with her this afternoon."

"Ah, Linda." That brought out his laugh crinkles again. "Allow me to introduce myself. I'm Pierre Seagrant, at your service."

"Are you French?" I hadn't detected any accent.

"Nee Peter Seagrant but I've always thought that as Pierre, I'd sell more paintings. As Linda may have told you, I'm a curious mixture of zee artiste, carnie and bon vivant." His eyes sparkled.

I laughed. "I think she did say something along those lines." Should I give him my real name? In for a penny in for a pound. I stuck my hand out. "Hi, I'm Onalee O'Conner."

He leaped up from his stool, grabbed my hand and kissed it. "Any friend of Linda's is a friend of mine."

Uh oh.

"Come. Allow me to show you some of her works," he said and scampered into the gallery.

Works? I would think that the only painting she'd do would be her lips. I followed at a more sedate pace.

Pierre stopped beside one of the pictures I'd admired earlier, a sweeping landscape of sand dunes and the lake. "This was a *plein aire* painting she did last summer at Sturgeon Bay." He studied me. "I'll bet you didn't realize your friend was so talented."

That was an understatement. "No, I honestly didn't. Does she go to your Tuesday night painting sessions?"

245

"Sadly, no. I think she finds them a bit, shall we say, amateurish? Coming here to paint in the afternoons when it's just she and I and our muses is more her style."

"So that's where she goes when I can't find her. Is she here most days?"

"Um, no. Maybe two or three days a week. Come, come, come. I want to show you another one of her paintings." He strode across the room.

"Oh, my gosh. Is this where she was the day of that awful murder?" I blurted out.

He halted. Then turned back to me, a puzzled look on his face. "No, she wasn't. I was out of town when that happened and the studio was closed."

"Oh, no. I was so hoping." I frowned. "I know she didn't kill Jonathon Richmond but, frankly, I'm worried about her."

He rounded on me. "Of course she didn't murder him. She has the soul of an artist, as you can see for yourself." He gestured at another lovely landscape apparently also done by the painting shrew. "She's a creator, not a killer."

"You're right," I said pausing. "But, then again, she slaughters those African trophy animals. I guess she is a bit of a walking contradiction."

"As her friend, you ought to realize that she accompanies her husband on his hunting forays, and she photographs the animals in their natural splendor. You must have seen her photos. It's been wonderful talking with you, but my heifer is calling me." He spun on his heel and strode back to his painting.

"See you next Tuesday?" I asked in a small voice.

"Yes, of course," he said with no friendly edge to his voice.

I showed myself out the door. Linda P. with the soul of an artist? How could that be? Even more surprising was that a warm, wonderful person like Pierre could be drawn in by her. There must be a small sliver of good in the woman. But did she have an alibi? Not that I could detect. Then again, I had one more stop I could make-Mimi's Fine Clothing on Sherwood Street in the Gas Light District.

I drove back into town and found a parking spot within two blocks of Mimi's. Even though it was still June, there were visitors frequenting our expensive stores, and many of them were carrying shopping bags. That was a good sign for our local merchants. I had never been in Mimi's but had window shopped there often. I was pretty sure I wasn't dressed like a typical Mimi's shopper, but this would have to do. Perhaps, some of the moneyed were eccentric and didn't always sport designer togs. It would certainly behoove the salespeople to treat everyone who entered the shop with dignity and respect. Head held high, I waltzed into Mimi's under the pretense of needing something with just the right panache, and I used that very word to Claudia, my shopper's assistant, for a special date. We looked through racks of haute couture madness. I struggled to keep an open mind but between the razzle-dazzle and the hauter-than-hell price tags I was having a dilly of a time keeping my focus.

To appease Claudia, I tried on a couple of sheer numbers with deep and plentiful slits. I couldn't bring myself to appear outside the fitting room where other shoppers freely roamed. And that's why I found Claudia ensconced in the small cubical with me.

She clasped her hands. "That bronze brings out the earthy tones in your skin. But you definitely need to wear your tallest stilettos with it."

She thinks I own stilettos? Maybe I am becoming a good actress. "Claudia, I came here because my friend Linda Lorian said I could find just what I need."

"I wondered. I've never seen you in here before."

"She's gotten some outfits in here that were simply divine."

"Yes she has. And, she looks stunning in them, don't you agree?"

"Oh yes. I'm glad she still likes to spend a frivolous afternoon here and there by coming here to shop. She's been so down lately." I lowered my voice. "You know, since all of that ugly business about the murder."

"Yes, that was hideous."

I watched Claudia closely. Did I detect a slight pursing of her lip? Could she too be less than thrilled with Linda P.? I went in for the kill. "I love Linda to death, but I know she can be a teensy bit demanding. I'll bet you may have noticed that side of her."

I had a feeling I was getting Claudia's attention. "I can't begin to count the number of times she's read me the riot act about something." Claudia was nodding along with my narrative now. "Come to think of it, I think I remember her ranting and raving about something she bought from you. I mean Mimi's of course."

"Oh yes. We have had some incidents," Claudia said, shaking her head.

I thought I had her on my side now. I leaned in closer to her. "I heard she's a suspect in that murder investigation."

"Really?"

"Really. What I'd like to know, though, is where she was at the time of the murder. Do you think she was here?"

"No, she wasn't. Like many of our local customers, she's here a lot but she definitely wasn't here that day. I remember, because we all talked about it."

"Then, I wonder where she was?" I thought a moment. "Claudia, as you probably have guessed, I'm not interested in buying a dress, and I'm not really a friend of Linda Lorian's.

"Who are you? Are you like an undercover cop or something?"

"No. I was the one who found Jonathon Richmond's body."

Her eyes widened. "I see. Do you think Mrs. Lorian was the killer?"

"I don't know. There are a number of us who are hoping so."

Claudia giggled. "This store would lose a ton of money if she was behind bars, but I think we'd all dance in the streets. At least I know I would."

Claudia helped me with the back zipper of the slinky bronze number and I climbed out of it.

"Oh, and another thing. I don't own any stilettos." I said as I pulled on my clothes.

Claudia grinned. "I was pretty sure you didn't. Remember, I'm a trained salesperson."

"Thank you for everything. I'll get out of your hair now."

"Don't worry. You made my day."

I drew the curtain aside and there stood Linda Pendleton Lorian.

"Oh dear." Visions of restraining orders filled my head.

"I knew that was your car out there. I told you to leave me alone," she screamed.

The other shoppers turned to gawk at us.

Claudia who had been behind me brushed past me. "Why hello, Mrs. Lorian. I'll be with you shortly." Then she turned to me. "Follow me up to the counter, ma'am. Will that be cash or charge today?"

Linda stood nonplused and watched as I followed Claudia to the sales counter.

Out of earshot, Claudia said, "I told you I was a trained professional." She grinned. "We have a back exit to the alley if you'd care to use it."

"I don't know how to thank you for all of this, Claudia."

"Nail her, if she's guilty. If she's not guilty, just keep driving her crazy. I couldn't ask for more than that."

251

"Thanks again. If you think of anything that might help, call me. Here's my card. I'm Onalee O'Conner, by the way." We shook hands and I slipped out the back door. Then, I walked back the two blocks to my car and drove home to Julian.

Chapter Thirty-one

A little after five o'clock that afternoon, I got a call from an exuberant Rosie. She was in town and at their hotel. She wanted me to bring my dress over so she could see it on me and decide if any alterations were needed.

I gathered up the dress and drove to the gracious old Waters' Edge Hotel. I had volunteered to help Rosie in any way she needed, but she and Burt had apparently handled all the arrangements themselves. However, if she'd have asked, I'd have told her the Waters' Edge would be an excellent choice.

Most of the inn consisted of a beautiful old Victorian-style facility built about one hundred years ago. But, the most recent owner had added a wing that complimented the old Dowager architecturally while providing modern amenities such as a swimming pool, hot tub and fitness room. Guest rooms had also been added in that wing, while the numerous tiny rooms in the other two wings had been combined into fewer, more spacious rooms and also updated.

Rosie's room was in the new wing on the fourth floor. I knocked, and she threw open the door. "Onalee, it's so great to see you again." This was the day for reunions, I guess. She hugged me warmly while I held the dress out at arm's length to keep it from being crushed in her embrace. "Oh, good, you've brought the dress. Come in. The hotel is wonderful. I've never stayed in such an elegant place before. Would you like a glass of lemonade on the deck? I'm surprised it's so hot out up here in June."

"Rosie, slow down." I grinned at her.

She giggled, "I guess I am a bit wound up, aren't I?"

"Save your energy for the wedding. And your bachelorette party. But lemonade sounds great."

I gently laid the dress out on the couch. We got our beverages and strolled out to the balcony overlooking the diamond studded bay. From this height, the lake seemed to be at our feet. We sipped our drinks and caught up on each other's lives over the past several months. Rosie had been talking about her badminton kids and then with no discernable segue said, "How about that dress?"

My mouthful of lemonade channeled into my windpipe and I dissolved into a paroxysm of coughing. Rosie watched me, concern flooding her eyes.

Hot Property

"Onalee, are you all right? Do you need help?" She'd raised her voice, possibly so that I could hear her over my gagging.

I couldn't talk, but I nodded my head.

She jumped to her feet. "Stand up and I'll perform the Heimlich maneuver on you."

I shook my head. "I'll be okay," I managed to squeak out.

That dress was going to kill me yet. After numerous throat clearings, I returned to my habitual, smoothly sophisticated demeanor.

Rosie was again seated across from me. "As I was about to say," She said, not one to let things slide, "Will you try the dress on for me?"

This time I was ready and said, "Sure," as I rose to my feet. Back in the living room, I gathered the dress, went into the bathroom, and changed into it. I looked at my frilly reflection in the full length mirror to make sure all of the parts were aligned correctly. Then, opened the door and there stood Rosie.

She clasped her hands. "Oh, Onalee, you look so pretty, it's perfect. It fits just right doesn't it? Is it comfortable?"

My smile might have been a bit too bright as I looked into those shiny button eyes of hers and said, "It's a great fit and it's a wonderful dress. I'm so happy to be your bridesmaid."

"All of you girls will look so lovely."

"Rosie, where are the other bridesmaids? I thought you were all coming together."

"No, they'll be here tomorrow for the party. The groomsmen will be up here too, with Burt. But of course, they'll be on their own."

*****

Rosie and I had dinner together at a restaurant in downtown Petoskey and then she went back to the hotel for an early bed time. Julian and I traipsed around the neighborhood, and we also were early hay hitters.

Chapter Thirty-two

The following morning I slept in a little in
anticipation of a long day and night. I hadn't
been to a lot of bachelorette parties but had
heard the stories. Where would we go? How hog
wild would it get? Would there be male
strippers? Rosie and I had had many a
conversation about just about everything, but
her thoughts on dudes sans duds had never come
up. Wherever we go, I decided, I'd drive
separately so that if the debauchery became
too debauched for this ingénue, I could exit
the scene.

Jules and I logged a good three mile run
and then had our breakfasts. One of my dog-
walker friends had agreed to pop in on Julian
throughout the day and tend to his needs.

As per Rosie's instructions, I drove back
to the hotel at 1:00 or pretty close to it.
The cloudless day was already scorching. Rosie
hadn't told me any details about the do, but
she had said to dress casually and bring my
swim suit. Today, the hotel was lively. On the
front lawn, there was a rousing game of
croquet being played by a group of children.

I jumped as a blood curdling scream rent the air. I quickly scanned the area in order to ascertain my needed course of action. Was flight or fight the appropriate response? Or, life-saving first aid? I soon located the source of the screaming. A diminutive croquet player had dropped to the ground and was beating on the grass with her fists. Another girl, laughing so hard she was hiccupping, looked up at me as I joined a circle of the participants.

"I just . . . s-sent her ball down the hill . . . and into the trees," the hiccupper explained to me. "I love this game," she said, pumping her fist.

Apparently, croquet is a passionate undertaking for these kids, I thought. Just then, out of the corner of my eye, I saw a bright yellow straw hat bobbing towards the group. Rosie, beaming, strode up to me.

"Onalee, you made it. Have you had a chance to meet the rest of your fellow bridal party yet?

I looked around but there was only Rosie, myself and the children. I think I may have allowed some confusion to cloud my face because Rosie began to explain.

"Onalee, this is Isabelle and Kelsey and Haley and Madison," she said, pointing to each of the girls. "Ladies, meet my dear friend,

Miss Onalee. She will be celebrating with us today and she's also in the wedding."

The four girls gave me cheery hellos before resuming their croquet. Rosie turned to me. "Burt and I have gotten very close to these kids since we began coaching them. When they heard about our wedding, they became so excited we decided to make them a part of it."

"So the groomsmen--"

"Yup. They're all about seven years old."

Zowie. Rosie and I stood on the sidelines watching until the game was finished. The hiccupper, Isabelle, maintained the lead almost until the end, then her ball was sent into the woods by Madison. Expecting the girl, such a fierce opponent, to stomp off after her ball, she surprised me by doubling over in another laughing jag.

"Girls, if you're ready to go to the beach, pick up the game and then we'll change into our suits," Rosie directed.

The girls scrambled, and soon the croquet set was back in its cart. A few minutes later, Rosie drove a van loaded with her chattering bridal attendants. At the beach, the girls were sweet and included me in their keep away ball games and sand castle construction projects. I wowed them with my ability to stand on my head in the water and my local knowledge of Petoskey stones.

We walked the beach, buried Isabelle to her neck and played in the waves. When my fingernails had a bluish tinge, I went in and sat on the blanket beside Rosie. Watching the girls play on a giant inner tube Rosie had brought for us, I asked, "What are Burt and the boys doing?"

"You know, manly things. Fishing, camping, swilling root beer and roasting hot dogs and s'mores over an open fire. They're at a campground out by a small lake. I think it's called Webber Lake."

Eventually, the sun tipped lower in the sky and we rounded up the kids, toweled them dry and packed them in the car. Back at the hotel, we took turns in the shower with Rosie getting first dibs and me second. Then while the girls washed up, we got the bachelorette party food ready.

The entrée choices were peanut butter and grape jelly sandwiches or ice cream sandwiches with sides of either corn chips or potato chips. The beverage choices were cherry Kool aid or pink lemonade. Madison required a special sandwich made with only grape jelly. After I placed that on her plate, she carefully made a small pile of corn chips and a separate stack of potato chips.

"I don't want any of my food touching each other," she explained when she saw me watching her.

Hot Property

Desert was a sundae bar with hot fudge, chocolate, butterscotch and cherry syrups. Other fixings included maraschino cherries, chocolate sprinkles, gummy worms, peanuts and mini marshmallows. The ice cream choices were plain old vanilla, chocolate and superman.

After my comparatively healthful dinner consisting of a peanut butter sandwich and side of corn chips, I stood in line at the sundae bar. I scooped up some vanilla ice cream then poured on a bit of hot fudge. What the hay, I said to myself, this is a bachelorette party, and everyone is supposed to be a bit decadent. I added a dollop of butter scotch topping.

Isabelle was in line behind me. She reached for the vanilla ice cream, then added a scoop of chocolate and then rounded out her bowl with a spoonful of superman. She poured on a generous amount of cherry syrup, followed by the chocolate, butterscotch and then the hot fudge. She dotted her masterpiece with chocolate sprinkles, a couple of the mini marshmallows and a fistful of the cherries. A gummy worm draped lazily over the top.

"What? No peanuts?" I asked.

"No room," she said grinning.

We all took our desserts out to our table on the balcony. Gummy worms were dangled down throats and chocolate smudges were appearing everywhere. Isabelle wielded her spoon and mashed her conglomeration of colors and flavors together until it was just the right consistency before taking her first bite.

"How is it?" I asked. I couldn't imagine what that kaleidoscope of flavors would taste like.

"It's a real pip," she said and shot a laughing look at Rosie.

"We've decided to bring back some of the old timey sayings," Rosie explained. Taking up her phone, she snapped pictures until the last spoon was laid down.

The girls washed up for the second time that day and climbed into their pajamas. Rosie started up the movie the kids had voted on and they snuggled in to watch it, chomping on popcorn. Meanwhile, I helped Rosie clean up the dessert detritus before leaving. "Rosie, are the kids going to sleep tonight after all that sugar?"

"Oh sure. You saw how much exercise they got today. I don't think they'll make it all the way through the movie."

We laughed. "Are you going to be okay alone with the kids?"

"The parents came up with us and will come to pick up the girls in another hour.

Meanwhile, they got a free day and night out without their children."

I gathered my wet swim suit and beach blanket. "This was a hoot, Rosie," I said.

"I knew you'd be a good sport about it, Onalee."

"Isn't there usually a wedding rehearsal?"

She looked thoughtful. "Yes, I believe there is, but our wedding will be a very simple affair. I think we'll just go over a couple of things at the last minute."

"How many guests will there be?"

"About a hundred. You'll know most of them. It'll be old home week, for you."

Great. It's always a good thing to be in ruffled finery in front of a lot of people you know.

Chapter Thirty-three

Rosie and Burt's wedding day dawned sunny and warm. After walking Julian, I met up with Rosie, the girls and two of the mothers for a brunch on the hotel's expansive veranda. Afterwards, we returned to Rosie's room and painted each other's nails. Rosie had a panoply of colors available, and most of my fellow bridesmaids made good use of the assortment. I opted for a conservative shade of pink for my fingertips. Unlike the girls, all of my fingers matched. My toe nails were already brushed with a sophisticated silver hue.

One of Burt's cousins had volunteered the use of his one hundred-year old farmhouse for the wedding, and we gathered up everyone's finery and proceeded to the site. It was nearly an hour's drive north to get to the tiny town of Bliss. Rosie had told me of their indecision about whether to be married in Bliss or Hell, Michigan. Then, the opportunity to use this farmhouse popped up and the issue was settled.

The house was situated atop a mammoth hill, and the van chugged up a steep drive. At the top, there were peeks of Lake Michigan in the distance. After the vehicle stopped, we climbed out and Rosie, with us in tow, walked over to the wooden porch steps. Reaching under the top step, she extracted a key.

After she opened the door, we all entered the living room. There were wood floors the color of honey with sunlight streaming through the windows. Multi-colored braided rugs were scattered around the room. The walls were a rich cream with oak crown moldings. The far wall was adorned with a fireplace, a fieldstone chimney and a rough-hewn wood mantle.

We had quit chattering and stared at the room. "Rosie, could this place be any cuter?" I breathed.

Smiling, she looked at me. "I don't think so. But let's check out the rest of the house," she said and led us through an archway into a cozy country kitchen.

"Are the owners here much? Everything looks so clean."

"I think they are. They just love it up here."

The girls had started chattering again and Isabelle and Kelsie peeled off to check out the rest of the house. I followed them and we explored a downstairs bathroom and three bedrooms on the second floor. The girls tumbled back down the stairs with me lagging behind. Everyone had gone outside and we found them around in back. Here the land, dotted with gnarled old apple trees, fell off gradually to a valley far below.

A breeze had sprung up and was tossing the tree branches against the sky.

"This is where we're going to have the wedding, girls," Rosie said. "The caterers will be here any minute now."

We turned our heads at the sound of a vehicle on the gravel drive. A couple of doors slammed, and a group of college-aged kids trooped into view with two women in their thirties. They inspected the site and then, working quickly, brought out chairs and tables from the truck. They began setting up the chairs in rows. Tables for the dinner were being set up behind them.

Meanwhile, the two older ladies walked up to our group. "You must be Rosie," the woman in the bright pink apron said, smiling. "I'm Cassie. After all of our phone calls, I feel like I've known you all my life." She hugged Rosie. "And this is my catering partner Carol."

After a round of introductions and more hugs, Cassie and Carol went back to their truck to begin unloading the food. We'd offered to help but had been told to go get ready for the wedding. Cassie was right, time was slipping away from us.

We traipsed back into the house and carried our dresses upstairs. Just then, through the window I saw another van rounding the last curve of the driveway. More car doors slammed, and soon little boys raced everywhere. "Girls, go ahead and get ready. I need to talk with Burt a minute," Rosie said.

I watched as Rosie caught up to him in the back yard. They embraced and then turned to watch the transformation of the orchard. They talked a bit and then, with a red-haired boy, the smallest of the group, walked hand in hand to the front of the seating area. Rosie and Burt talked to the boy, occasionally pointing out things to him and then they all walked back towards the house. A few minutes later, Rosie, looking a bit flushed, was back with us. Then she hoisted the plastic bag covering her dress and retreated to the bathroom.

I was ready by this time and helped some of the others with the zippers that ran up the backs of all of our frocks. The girls all had gowns that were like mine but in mint green, soft blue, creamy yellow and circus peanut orange. They looked adorable.

Rosie emerged in a flowing, watery blue linen dress. It was perfect.

"You look so pretty," I said, tears welling up.

Under her breath she said, "Hells bells, Onalee. Don't get all teary-eyed on me."

I swiped my face. "Okay, Ma'am."

"Miss Rosie? Are the boys getting dressed up, too?"

Rosie turned to the little blond girl, "Yup. They're changing in the van. They say it's bad luck for the groom to see the bride before the wedding, Kelsie."

"Yeah, I know. My mom told me about that."

Out the open window we could see the guests arriving and being escorted to their seats by a couple of badminton players from one of the Grosse Pointe clubs. Hammered dulcimer music wafted in on the breeze.

The girls, led by Isabelle, swarmed Rosie. "Can we decide on the maid of honor, now? Please?" Isabelle wheedled, smiling up at Rosie.

"What do you think I brought this deck of cards for? Everyone has an even chance at it. I want you each to draw a card and the one with the highest card will be my maid of honor. Aces will be highest and then king, queen, right down the line. If two of you have the same card, you can each draw another one to break the tie. Ready?"

Hot Property

The girls, who had lined up beside each other, all nodded, solemnly. Rosie held the deck out to each one of them and they selected a card. I was standing to one side and wasn't offered a card. It's not that I was jealous or wanted to be the maid of honor. I was, after all, above that sort of petty, small mindedness. But, I did wonder what my role in this production would be.

After each girl selected her card, Rosie said, "Does anyone have a two?" She was playing the crowd. "No? A three?" Finally, Maddy raised her hand when Rosie got to seven. There was, of course, a tie, with a playoff and the maid of honor tribute was bestowed on Haley. She was the shiest of the four girls and it was a tip top outcome, in my opinion. I think the other girls were happy for her as well.

"Girls, you'll all line up to walk down the aisle, in that order, low card to high card. Finally, Rosie turned to me. "As you can see, Onalee, there's one small detail I haven't explained to you yet."

Her worried expression put me on my guard. "Oh?"

"It's a matter of balance. At least, that's what Burt and I thought. I hope you won't mind."

"Spit it out, Madam Bride."

"The girls and boys are all about the same size. So, we've decided that the girls would all be my bridesmaids. And you, dear friend, are going to be my flower girl."

Chapter Thirty-four

And so it was that I found myself in a cloud of pink chiffon, trailing slowly after Sanjay, Burt's best friend and ring bearer, down the aisle. On both sides of me was a sea of familiar faces. At the end of the rows of chairs, I turned to the left and joined the little bridesmaids who were standing and facing the audience.

Everyone got to their feet as Rosie paraded down the aisle. She took her place beside us and the red haired boy walked over to a podium. It took him a minute while he scrambled up on a stool, then he began to speak in a small, quivery voice. "Dearly beloved, we are gathered," I missed some of what he said as I realized that Rosie and Burt were going to take their vows before this half-pint pastor. A few minutes later, he pronounced, "Ladies and gentlemen, may I present Rosie Ryder and Burt McMillan, husband and wife. Rosie and Burt, holding hands, beamed at the audience, then they swept up the aisle followed by pairs of bridal attendants including Sanjay and I.

There was no assigned seating at the banquet tables situated under a large white tent. The dinner buffet included numerous Indian dishes along with trays full of chicken, roast beef, cheesy potatoes and a tossed salad made with spring greens, candied pecans and cherries. In honor of Burt, the wedding cake had been scrapped in favor of praline pecan, raspberry swirl and triple chocolate cheese cakes. I noticed many of the guests chose a slice of each.

I sat with my former ladies doubles partner, Sandy and her new friend, Ian. Even without a Scottish accent, Ian would have been utterly charming. He got up to refill our wine glasses so Sandy and I had a few minutes to talk. "He's a cutie," I said. "But how is he—"

"Great!" she said, following my train of thought.

"He knows just where to put the bird."

"And?"

"We won the senior mid-western mixed-doubles tournament in Milwaukee last month."

I cleared my throat in a meaningful way. "How old did you say he was?"

She giggled. "Forty-three. I know I have no right—"

Hot Property

Ian set our wine glasses in front of us and looked questioningly at Sandy. "What don't you have a right to, Hon?"

She looked up at him, "When I was thirty-five and Onalee was forty-one, we divided up all the men in the world. I got everyone under the age of forty and she got all of you who are forty and older. So, technically, you're one of hers and we shouldn't be together."

"Don't we men get some say in this?" he asked.

"No," I answered simply.

"But, about a year ago, she threw all of the married guys into my group, so I guess I can't complain. Of course, since you're not married, I'm not entitled to you that way, either." Sandy added.

Ian threw his arm around Sandy. "I'm going to lodge a formal protest. I just met you Onalee, and already you're ruining my future. Who would think that a forty-something flower girl in pink ruffles would be so tough."

I looked at the two of them sitting so happily together. Maybe it was those two slices of cheesecake talking, but I felt expansive and said, "I can't make any promises, but I will take your protest under advisement, young man."

I wondered around to talk with some of my other badminton friends. I saw the little red-haired preacher sitting by Isabelle.

"Do you want to see my pocket card?" He dug it out and handed it over to her. "Burt told me that it was $11.99 with free shipping and handling," he added.

Isabelle looked up at me and grinned. Then she studied the card. "Zackary G. Farrow, ordained minister of the Church of Christian Life." she read. "Cool, eh?" She asked.

I nodded my head. "Very impressive. You did a bang-up job, Reverend Farrow." Then I moved on. Rosie and Burt were just ahead.

"Great wedding, you two," I hugged each of them. Are you going on a honey moon?"

Rosie and Burt looked at each other. "Burt is taking me to Paradise. But, just for a couple of days. Then next spring we're going to see the Thomas and the Uber cups in Indonesia."

"You're talking about the picturesque town of Paradise in the Upper Peninsula, right?"

"Of course. Remember our ages, Onalee."

"And then the Thomas and Uber Cups? Wow." The top men's and women's badminton tournaments in the world were probably on every badminton player's bucket list.

Hot Property

"Onalee, you look a bit sad. Are you okay?" Burt asked.

I sighed. "I'm fine. I just miss badminton so much. The closest place to play is about three hours from my house. But, it has been wonderful to see everyone." I looked around at my friends from England, Denmark, Germany, India, Jamaica, and Canada.

Burt smiled. "I know they call this God's country up here and it is beautiful. But if there is no badminton, can it really be that hallowed?"

"Now, Burt, this is Onalee's home now. Don't make her feel bad," Rosie chided.

"Yeah, Burt. You'll make me so upset that you'll drive me to buy one of those backyard sets for $7.99."

"Okay, Onalee, I'll back off," Burt said, laughing.

The party lasted for a couple of more hours then we said farewell to Rosie and Burt, who were going to Mackinaw Island, to spend their first night together. I drove home in time for Julian's evening walk. It was late, and our evening constitutional was generally quite short. I elected to stay suited up in my flower girl outfit rather than taking the time to change into something more suitable. After all, who would see me at this time of night?

Chapter Thirty-five

Julian and I high-stepped off my porch and into the moonless night. It was still about 70 degrees. Back in the day, when I was just a sprout, we were lucky to have one night per summer that was temperate. Already this hot June, we'd had a spate of them. A slight breeze ruffled my hair. Julian trotted along and I struggled to keep up in my flower girl footwear. Julian was a guy who was particular about his bathrooms, and I knew we'd have to walk at least a couple of blocks. I probably should have taken the time to change into better walking shoes, I thought as I clopped down the street. Our neighborhood doesn't have sidewalks, so we all use the road for our forays.

We finally made it to one of his favorite spots, a large maple tree. But, of course the process involves a great deal of sniffing. As he busied himself with his examination, I tried to pick out a few constellations in the night sky.

A car approached us but since I was on the other side of the street from its path, I didn't bother to move over. Although we don't have very much traffic, I generally watch, making sure the driver sees me rather than a text message.

So it was, that I kept an eye on the oncoming car. Julian was still in sniffing mode when all of a sudden the car veered towards me, tires screeching. It was bearing down on me. Right at me. There was no time. I dove to the side of the road. The car whooshed past me as I slammed into the ground. Julian was barking and someone was yelling. I had to get up. What if that car came back for me? But, I couldn't breathe. Julian, whimpering, nudged me with his nose. Suddenly a man appeared. Julian wheeled to face him, a growl rumbling in his chest.

"Lady. Are you all right? Easy, boy," he said, eyeing Julian. "I called 9-1-1. That guy was nuts." He continued to stare at me.

I tried to talk but only wheezed. I must have gotten the wind knocked out of me.

"Are you okay?" He repeated.

Julian, not liking the man's entreaties, growled louder.

I nodded and finally I managed to utter, "I'm fine. Julian, it's okay." I rolled to a sitting position as the sound of sirens tore through the night. Julian backed down and turned his attention back to me. "I'm so glad you're okay, boy," I said hugging him.

"Yeah, you both could've been killed by that maniac."

A police car slammed to a stop a few feet away from where I still sat on the ground. Leaving the car running, a patrolman climbed out and strode directly over to me. "Are you okay, ma'am?"

"Yeah, I'm fine." I started to get to my feet.

The officer reached out to steady me as Julian growled. "Take it easy, there's no rush." He looked closely at my face. Apparently, I was at least semi-hunky dory because he stepped away from my side. "What happened here?" The policeman looked back and forth between the man and myself.

A second car motored up and Detective Costas arrived. "Ms. O'Conner? Is that you? Are you okay?" He hurried over and scanned me from head to toe with a concerned look on his face. "You're shaking."

"Hi. I'm all right. It was just scary." Julian remained on guard beside me but, oddly, he didn't growl at the detective.

"She could've been smashed into a grease spot by that crazy driver."

Costas turned to him, "Who are you, sir?"

"I'm the guy who called 9-1-1. Name's Phillip Miley. I saw the whole thing."

278

Hot Property

"What happened, Mr. Miley?"

He pointed at me with his thumb. "She was walking that dog. I had noticed her because when she stepped under the street light she looked like a . . . sawed off flamingo. Anywho, she and the dog had stopped, I guess he needed to do his business. This parked car started up and came down the road. It looked to me like it was gunning for her. She did this fantastic leap. I'm telling you, it looked like a giant pink puff ball arcing across the stars. I don't think I'll forget that sight as long as I live."

Sawed off flamingo, indeed. I'd forgotten about my flower girl finery. It wouldn't have killed me to have taken five minutes to change before going out tonight. Costas gave me a sidelong glance. I'm pretty sure that I saw twitching lips but to his credit, he didn't laugh.

"Did you get the license plate or see the type of car it was?" Costas asked, remaining beside me."

"No. It all happened too fast."

"What direction was the car going?"

"It was parked over there," Miley said, pointing in the direction of my house. "After it tried to mow her down, it continued on down the road, heading north."

279

"Please give your name, telephone number and address to my officer. I need to get her back to her house. One more thing, what were you doing out at this time of night?"

"I am staying with friends in the neighborhood. It was a beautiful night so I decided to take a little walk."

"I'm glad you were here. You undoubtedly saved her life."

Costas turned back to me. "Why don't you and the dog hop into my car."

"Thanks, Mr. Miley," I grudgingly called over to him. He probably did save my life even though his crass remarks almost caused death by humiliation. Then to Detective Costas I said, "Would you mind, I'd rather walk, I think."

He looked at me again. "You're sure?"

"Yeah."

"Okay. Just one sec." Costas strode over and shut his car off. Then as he walked Julian and me back home he asked me what I remembered of the incident. It had been basically as the guy had described it, though I took umbrage at the giant pink puff ball analogy. I hadn't noticed the parked car. It had happened too fast for me, and I had no idea of the make or color of the vehicle. All I knew for sure was that it was a sedan of some kind and not a compact.

"That seems like a nice dog you've got there."

"Thanks. He's my neighbor's dog but you're right, he's wonderful." The night didn't seem real to me, and Costas making small talk just added to that other-worldly sensation.

"Were you at a party tonight? You look nice."

I whirled around to look at him but he seemed earnest. "I was in a wedding."

"Ah, that explains it. That's the fluffiest dress I've ever seen."

He saw my frown.

"But on you it's nice. It works." He smiled.

"Thanks and I appreciate you walking me home."

At my door, Costas offered to search through the house to make sure no one was there. I would have taken him up on it if I hadn't had Julian with me, but I knew he'd immediately react if there were any intruders.

A few minutes later as I removed my torn and battle-scarred frock, it hit me that Rosie had been wrong about one thing, this was not a dress I'd ever wear again.

Chapter Thirty-six

After this forever day I washed up, brushed my teeth, examined my contused everything, and then tottered off to bed. I was so tired and sooo wide awake. As I lay there, I noticed creaks and groans in the house I'd never heard before. More than once, as I tossed and turned, I woke poor Julian up. Sometime before dawn, I finally drifted off to a nightmarish sleep.

The following day, I slept in a bit as wind-driven rain pelted my windows. It was cozy, and I was beginning to feel safe again. It was not a time to rush myself. I slowly got to my feet, feeling all of my bruises. I lumbered into the kitchen, put a pot of coffee on and heated a muffin in my microwave. Then I took my breakfast back to bed and read my book through two cups of coffee.

Finally, I got up, dressed and snapped Julian's leash on. He walked out the door but halted at the edge of the porch. I tugged on his leach, but he planted his front paws and refused to move. I pulled a little harder, and he answered my challenge by sitting back on his haunches.

"Julian. Come." I said authoritatively. He answered me this time by lying down.

Maybe reasoning with him would work. "Julian, I know it's miserable out but haven't you ever heard that old saying, 'A dog's gotta do what a dog's gotta do?'"

He laid his head on his paws but watched me, waiting to see what other persuasive techniques I could dig up. I sighed. Finally after fifteen minutes or so of this stalemate, punctuated by treats, AKA bribes, more leash tuggings, pleadings and even pronouncements such as no swimming for a week, I gave up. We turned around and went inside. In a final act of desperation, I called Mrs. Stirnaman.

"Oh, sweetie. He does need to stick to a regular schedule. I neglected to tell you of his little idiosyncrasy. Go back outside and open your car door for him. I know it's a bit of an imposition, but on stormy days like today, he expects to be driven over to the bike path. He will concede to a brief walk then. And by the way, Onalee, that handsome Dr. Parks asked about you this morning. Can you pop by on Tuesday about 9:00 a.m. during his rounds?"

*****

Just as Mrs. S. said, as soon as I opened the passenger side door, Julian ran down the porch stairs and leapt into the car.

The rain quit during the late morning and the sun blazed.

I had work I could do but instead lazed around at the beach as if I hadn't a care in the world. The wedding had been a welcome break from all of the murder and mayhem swirling around me, but last night had brought it all back. As I swam on my back, I thought about the rest of my Sunday. I'd have a nice quiet dinner on my deck, perhaps sipping a small glass of wine as dusk cloaked Northern Michigan.

I showered, took Julian for his walk and then checked my messages. Marti had called three times.

"Hi, On. It's me. Call me as soon as you get in."

Then, "Where the heck are you? I called your cell phone too, but you didn't pick up." A few minutes later, "Come on. Call me puleeze!"

I punched in her number. "Hi Marti."

"Could you have been any slower? I'm going to permanently attach a cell phone to your hip. Listen. If I tell you something, you've got to promise not to tell anyone, no matter what. Okay?"

"I don't know. What's this about?"

"Come on. You've got to trust me on this. We don't have much time. Do you promise?"

"Okay, I guess. I promise. But I'm telling you right now, I don't like it."

"Whatever. Anyway, Frank called me today and was all upset about Amber's death. Seems Amber had come to Northern Michigan because of him. She was the baby sister of a good friend of his in college. Frank and Amber dated for a while."

"What? Marti, this is huge. We have got to tell this to the police."

"No. Don't you see? This might implicate him in her death too."

"Exactly. Which is why I say we need to go right to the police on this."

"You promised, On," she said dismissively. Now what I want you to do is this. He's not home and should be gone for a few more hours, from what he said. I want you to go out to his house and nose around. See if you find anything that might incriminate him."

"Listen, Perry Mason. If he's innocent, the cops won't find anything. Let's let them do it."

"No. Of course, we know he's innocent. But it won't hurt for you to double-check. He hides a key under the third step of his house."

We argued for a while longer, but in the end, Marti cajoled until I gave in.

Chapter Thirty-seven

Marti had also pleaded with me to not take Julian, because Frank's dog would probably be there and wouldn't tolerate another dog in his territory. I rummaged around in my purse until I found my Swiss army knife and stuck that in the pocket of my shorts. Geesh, it didn't go very far into said pocket before it clunked into my stakeout jar of extra hot curry powder. What the hay. There was no time to fish everything out. I just wanted to get this cockamamie errand over with and get back to my nest.

I made the now-familiar drive to Frank's neighborhood, in good time. Before turning up the driveway, I glanced in the rearview mirror, making sure no one saw me pull in. The roar of my tires on the gravel grated on my nerves as I made my way up to the house. This was exactly the kind of thing that always drove me crazy when those over-cajonied women private investigators go breaking and entering places. It's way too scary. And here, thanks to Marti, I was doing it.

My eyes caught a sudden movement behind one of Frank's trees. "Oh dear God!" Chills shot down my legs and lodged in my toes. Suddenly, two squirrels darted out, chasing each other across the yard. That must be what I saw. How would Marti ever be able to pay back the two years of my life that this little adventure was costing me?

I drove in the rest of the way and turned the car around in readiness for a rapid get-away. Then I climbed out and slunk to the house. Everything was still. No gravel crunched on the drive behind me. Far below, and off to the right, the condos shimmered in the evening sun. I imagine they were open for showings earlier in the day but the sales office was probably closed by now. Everything was peaceful and quiet.

The key was ridiculously easy to find. Wasn't Frank at all concerned about break-ins? I had given thought to this caper all the way out here. It seemed that the smartest and most efficient way to search the house would be to start in the upstairs and work my way down. Most likely, things of a more personal nature would be in the bedroom.

Also, the longer I was in the house, the better chance I had of running into Frank. If I heard his car there might be time to slip outside, especially if I were downstairs. Then, I'd let him find me knocking at his front door as he drove up. This was the best escape plan I could muster, since there was only one long driveway.

My story would be that Marti was worried and had sent me. Then, without arousing any undue suspicions, I'd make my excuses and leave, keeping my fingers curled around my Swiss army knife as I slid past him. I was pleased at how well I had covered all of the contingencies, despite the riskiness of these ops.

No dog barked as I let myself in. Frank must have Caesar with him. Approaching the stairway, a sense of dread overcame me. Maybe I should start with the kitchen. After all, it wouldn't be wise to be trapped on the second floor with only one exit route. No. Stick to the plan. I forced myself to trudge up the long steep stairway to the loft.

Just as before, everything was tidy. It even looked freshly dusted. What a guy. Works full time, possibly commits a spot of arson, snuffs out a couple of marks on the side, all the while keeping an orderly abode. Move over, Martha Stewart.

In his bedroom, I reached between his mattress and box springs and peeped beneath his bed. Then I looked through each of his dresser drawers. So far, all I knew for sure was that he was another boxers guy. His clothes closet held assorted jeans and slacks on the right side and numerous tee shirts and long sleeve shirts, sorted by color, on the left. An upper shelf was loaded with sweaters and sweatshirts, all neatly folded. I pulled a chair over, clambered up on it and checked between all of them. Still nothing. Just as Marti had said, "The guy is a good dresser."

I stepped down and put the chair back, then moved over to his desk. In a side drawer he kept receipts of all of his paid bills in hanging file folders. There seemed to be just the usual utility and other household bills. So far I was getting a good lesson in how to be organized.

I checked the top drawer. Toward the back was a packet of pictures. I quickly shuffled through them. Most of them seemed to be scenes around Northern Michigan in the winter.

Uh oh, pay dirt. A picture of Frank and Amber, on skis, leaning on their poles, and grinning at the camera. So they had spent time together. I turned it over. No notation on the back. The date on the photo was last winter. Hmm. The rest of the pictures were more scenery shots.

By now, the bedroom was completely tossed. Interesting. I'm beginning to utter thoughts in private eye lingo. Very good. Or is it? The recently tossed bedroom might belong to a killer who could return at any moment, and be ever so slightly peeved at said "tossing".

Hot Property

I scampered to the bathroom and searched
rapidly through standard toiletries. No ring
around Frank's tub, uh, uh. No soap film in
the sink. Had he been tipped off to a possible
inspection? Were things just a lit-tle too
clean? Or were these the natural suspicions of
the chronically under-tidy? A quick glance at
my watch, revealed I'd been here about ten
minutes. Too long. On the other hand, there
was still no movement in the driveway.

I pondered as I searched. Yes, there
now proof of a connection between Frank and
Amber. But, a hunch was forming in my craw and
if I was right, then he was not the guilty
party. Tomorrow, I'd nose around and ask a few
more questions.

I bounded down the stairs and into the
kitchen. Ha. Busted. A dirty coffee cup sat on
the kitchen table with a coffee ring at the
bottom. Also last night's newspaper was strewn
on the counter, although all of the other
dishes were neatly stacked in the dish
drainer. I glanced at the refrigerator. A
picture of Frank with his arm slung around
Marti was held in place by two small magnets.
Was Marti just his "Honey du Jour" or was he
as smitten with her as she seemed to be with
him?

The inside of the refrigerator held a
couple of beers and part of a roast. Wonder
Boy also cooks. Further investigations

291

revealed brown bread rather than white, a large plastic container of salad greens and a quart of fresh strawberries. Unless he turns out to be the neighborhood killer/arsonist, Marti better snare this lad. A guy who eats his veggies. Maybe even if he did commit a bit of arson, just as long as he stopped shy of murder. Extreme circumstances may have led to the fires and the power of a strong woman to change a man for the better should never be underestimated.

I also looked behind the fridge and ran a long knife underneath, hoping to detect stray papers. Nothing. I popped open cabinets and the broom closet, even the oven. A search of the rest of the house turned up no additional evidence. I went outside, breathing a sigh of relief to be done with the B and E. The storage shed also yielded nothing except more damning evidence of organization. There were no accelerants, other than a half empty two-gallon can of gasoline next to the lawnmower.

I searched the bushes. Could he have buried anything suspicious? I didn't find any evidence of fresh digging anywhere. Off near the condos I caught sight of movement. A car was speeding up the driveway to Whispering Pines. I probably wasn't visible from down there but ducked behind a bush anyway. What would a car be doing there at 7:00 p.m.? Then again, there are often evening showings of properties, especially with our long hours of summer daylight.

The car door opened and a lone figure jumped out, popped open the trunk and began removing what looked to be a large container. Uh oh! The nearest condo unit was then opened and the can was taken inside.

Should I stay here and make sure of what I was seeing or call the police and fire department? Could I even move? My mind raced as my fingers fumbled for my cell phone. But, by the time the police got here, it might be too late. I pushed 9-1-1 and raced towards my car. My breath was coming in gasps as I quickly outlined the situation for the dispatcher. I started the Honda and careened down the driveway and onto the road.

If I waited for help, it could take them fifteen to twenty minutes to respond to this remote location in the county. By then, the killer would probably be long gone. I had to do it myself. I sped to the driveway of the condos and slammed to a halt. I jumped out of the car, leaving the door open to avoid unnecessary noise. If I ran the rest of the way, maybe I'd maintain the element of surprise.

The person was still in the condo as far as I could tell. The only weapon I had was my Swiss army knife. Would that be enough or did she have a gun? The doors of all of the units were open. I could see flames in the two units to the far left. The arsonist must be working her way down the project, setting fire to each unit. With a little luck, I could dash into a unit before she got that far, and attack her when she opened the door. I'd have the element of surprise on my side and could probably at least delay her until help arrived.

Gripping my knife with the longest, sharpest blade extended, I slunk inside. I detected a faint odor of smoke and gasoline as the door slammed shut behind me.

Chapter Thirty-eight

Guess I was wrong about the perp's
whereabouts. And my earlier question about
weapons was answered by the gun pointing
disturbingly close to where my heart
ricocheted around my chest cavity. Trapped!
And from the crackling noise I heard, a fire
was already started in the master bedroom,
though the door was closed.

"Well if it isn't Super Sleuth, O'Conner.
I've got to hand it to you. How in the world
did you know I was here?"

"I had a hunch." I said, trying to catch my
breath and not willing to tell her what I had
been doing just moments ago. "I thought you
said you were never involved with Jonathon.
'Just friends' you said. I guess you lied
about that, eh?"

"You think I killed Jonathon?" she asked,
her voice dripping with sarcasm.

"Yeah. Unless you're really into bonfires.
So, let me guess, because you and he had been
friends for so long, when you finally became
lovers, you thought it would be different for
you. Right? Don't you know that those skirt

chasers never change? Didn't I tell you about my last disastrous relationship with the Odious Tim?" I was going for the palsy-walsy approach. I didn't have anything to lose since she obviously knew how to shoot a gun, and I was only about six feet downwind from her. "Marissa, tell me. Did he dump you for Linda P?"

Her laugh was grim. "Oh yes. But it was even uglier than that. He dumped me for that bitch but he was also screwing Susie Sex-cretary on the side. In fact, I think he was doing her at the same time he was pledging his undying love for me." Another little unpleasant chortle slid past her lips. "Well I guess it wasn't UN-dying love, after all, was it?"

"No, I guess not, but hey, great pun, Marissa. I've always loved your sense of humor." I held up a hand between my heart and her gun. Not that it would do any good, but I just had to do it. "I don't blame you for being ticked off. How could he go for someone as low class as Linda P? So, you dumped my buddy Rob Darnell for Jonathon, I'm guessing. I remember that day in the Park Garden, when he basically said you'd dumped him. I always wondered why you'd called it off with such a great guy."

"Yes, you know 'a woman in love'." She shrugged her shoulders.

"Oh yeah. Been there. Anyway, I'm guessing you shot Amber, too, right?"

"You are so perceptive, Onalee. As stupid as she was, that little whore was close to figuring it out. I could just tell. She had to go."

"Gees, I would have thought Linda P. would have been at the top of your hit list."

She grinned at me. "We could have been great friends if this hadn't all happened. You and I think a lot alike."

Hmmmph, that was nice to hear. On the other hand, maybe the buddy system would work here.

"But, no, looks like I won't get a crack at Linda P. This is it for my little crime spree." She shook her head, eyes glittering wildly. Then, she continued. "Jon broke my heart but all I was to him was just another notch on his belt." She shook her head. "That was after years and years of being close friends. He was my best friend." She glared at me. "You can't treat people that way."

"No, you're right," I said placatingly. "You can't, or at least you shouldn't. But listen, we really need to get out of here. It sounds to me like there's a fire behind that closed door. Anyway, don't worry, your secret is safe with me. I can definitely understand why you did it." I attempted a big toothy grin, though this was undoubtedly one of those times when an observer would say of me, 'The smile didn't reach her eyes.'" I continued, "In fact I might even hire your services someday."

She broke out in another laugh, this one sounding more natural. "Oh, Onalee, I am going to hate to have to do it, but of course, I'm going to have to kill you, too. Would you mind handing over that knife you're clutching? Nice and easy. Just slide it along the floor towards me. Slowly. Blade towards you."

I was afraid of this. "One more question. Did you set the other fire, too?"

"No way. What do you think I am?" she said self-righteously. "I'd guess it was that stupid tree-hugger guy, Frank, but I don't know. He caused a lot of trouble for us with his protests and getting everybody all riled up. Anyway, after this fire, hopefully they'll blame him for everything. Then I can go back to my nice quiet life. Now, quit stalling around and give me that knife. I have to get going."

"Wait. One more question?"

"You're out of time, Onalee."

I ploughed on. "Was it you who tried to run me over last night."

A smile danced on her lips. "Yes it was. The problem was that I had to be so careful

298

not to hurt that beautiful dog. I waited until he was safely out of the way and then I didn't have as clear of a shot at you." She shook her head. "It doesn't matter. I couldn't live with myself if I hurt a dog."

"My mom always said, 'There's something wrong with people who don't like dogs'. Speaking of which, I need to get back for Julian's last walk of the evening."

She chuckled. "Nice try, Onalee. Now, like I said, hand over the knife."

I leaned down and pushed the knife gently towards her. She eyed it.

"How cute. I've never seen a pink Swiss army knife." Keeping the gun pointed in my direction and her eyes on me, she reached for the knife. "I'm going to keep it and every time I use it, I'll think of you."

"As well you should. That knife cost me a pretty penny. Oh, and FYI, I never used the toothpick attachment, so there are no germs on it. You don't have to worry." No, I was the one who had to worry. Plenty. This was a pretty pickle I was in. I was weaponless while she had a gun. What could I do? Then again. . . I might have one chance left but I needed to focus and not give in to my growing panic.

"As much fun as this has been, we need to wrap things up, here. I want you to scurry

over and open that door to the master
bedroom."

Oh no. "Marissa. I called the police and
they're on their way. It's over. Besides, I
don't like fires, actually."

"Yeah right, you called the police. I can't
get cell phone service out here, how could
you? Knowing you, I'll bet you wanted to
capture the big bad killer all by yourself."
She bared her teeth at me. "Anyway, we need to
wrap this up."

"Honestly, my phone does work. Look, I'll
show you." I started to reach into my pocket.

"Stop." She commanded. "Keep your hands
where I can see them." She waved her gun at
me. "I'm losing patience and you don't want me
to do that. Now come on. Move it."

I could hear the fire crackling louder
behind the door. With her pistol prodding me
in the back, I shambled towards it. She was
following directly behind me. I must have cut
quite a pathetic figure, head hanging down in
defeat, no longer the proud appraiser/amateur
sleuth. I slowly inched my hands downwards and
eventually found my pockets. If I could just
get the top off without her knowing it. I trod
ahead, even slower, giving myself a few extra
moments. My thumb and forefinger worked
feverishly within the confines of the pocket
of my shorts.

Hot Property

"Hurry up, or you'll soon feel the sting of a bullet in your leg. Followed by one in your other leg and you'll die a slow, agonizing death. If you're a good girl, I'll allow you to have a nice, quick departure."

The screw cap was off. Now for the flip top, sprinkling cap. It popped. I had to wait for my chance, if it came. They say you always have at least one. Hopefully it hadn't already come and I'd missed it. I was at the door. I reached for the knob. It was hot. "Ow." My hand shot back.

"Onalee. Open the door. Now," she snarled.

Gritting my teeth, I gave the knob a quick twist and pushed the door open. Dancing flames sprang towards us as oxygen rushed through the open doorway.

Bam! Something dropped to the floor from the fire. I felt Marissa step back a bit, momentarily distracted. My fist closed around the jar of peppery curry powder and I flung it at her eyes. I missed, but at least she sneezed. I swung at her, and the gun flew from her hand and into the flames. I bolted for the front door, grabbing for it. She caught up to me. Marissa was taller and had about ten pounds on me, but at least it seemed as though she had also dropped the knife.

We grasped at each other's hair, clothes, anything we could get our hands on. Her nails raked along my arm and I yelped from the pain. Flames licked just a few feet away from us, and the acrid smoke made us both gag. I swung again, blindly, and felt my fist connect somewhere. She fell away.

"You bitch!" She was back on me. Her hands grasped my neck. "You'll burn in here and they'll never know."

She was so strong. Heaving my arms up, I tried to break her hold. Nothing worked. She laughed hysterically. The flames roared closer. Smoke. Everywhere now. Blinding me. She grasped my neck harder, choking me. I brought my leg up and stomped with everything I had on her foot. Her grip loosened and I flung open the door.

Gasping. Wheezing. The entire building was in flames now as I skittered away. The sound of approaching sirens suddenly filled the air. Marissa stumbled out of the inferno. She pivoted, gazed at me and then her eyes riveted in the direction of the sirens. Abruptly, she turned and careened toward her car.

I tore after her. She was almost to the vehicle. Out of options, I flew at her legs. She was not going to get away. She tumbled down on top of me and, again, we rolled around, scratching and punching at each other. With her mega-nails, I got the worst of it, but if I could just hold on for a few more minutes. . . . It was taking forever for those emergency vehicles to get here. Then, suddenly, a car barreled toward us. Police flew out of car doors and arms reached in to the melee and pulled us apart.

"She's crazy." Marissa screamed, looking up at the cops. "Arrest her. She burned this place down and tried to kill me."

"What? No." I wheezed and then had a coughing jag. "I . . . I saw her setting fires and tried to stop her."

Detective Camille Costas looked back and forth between us.

"Detective?" The voice came from a police officer rummaging through Marissa's car. "I can smell accelerant in this car, and the registration says it belongs to Miss Martin." At that, Marissa scrambled to her feet and tried to run, but a young officer quickly caught up to her. She was thrown to the ground, then handcuffed and led back towards us. I watched as they informed Marissa of her rights. After she shot me a venomous look, they put her in the back seat of the police car.

For a few moments I just sat, stunned. Fire truck after fire truck came. Water poured from their hoses onto the blaze. The building was engulfed and would burn to the ground. I thought of being trapped in that burning building and shivered.

I'd seen enough, I wanted to go home. Costas strode over and reached out a hand to help me as I struggled to get to my feet.

"Take it easy, Ms. O'Conner. You look like you tangled with a wolverine. How do you feel?"

What must I look like? He kept peering at me with a concerned look on his face and no hint of his usual smirk.

Startled, I looked up at him. He was actually smiling at me.

Epilogue

As the days passed, one following another, details emerged about Marissa. She had been born Maria Martino and raised in Southwest Detroit. About the time her favorite brother, Angel, joined a neighborhood gang, she was accepted to Cass Tech, a school for the brightest students in the city. There, she rose to the top of her class, determined to better herself. Meanwhile, Angel took it upon himself to teach her street smarts. By graduation, she'd earned a full ride scholarship to Wayne State University, and could shoot the eye out of a beanie baby with a hand gun at twenty yards.

As an adult, selling real estate, she'd applied for and been granted a concealed weapons permit. She often carried a pistol for personal safety. Unbeknownst to yours truly, the police had found this out in their investigations of the R & L staff, but she was one of four brokers there with concealed weapons permits. No one knew that Jon and Marissa were involved though Amber may have suspected it.

The police had checked the ballistics of all of the pistols belonging to the R & L group, and none of them had matched the bullets from the murder victims. The current theory was that Marissa could have easily obtained a second gun to use as the murder weapon from her brother's illicit contacts. Neither she nor Angel are talking.

Meanwhile it appears that Frank, AKA, Frankie the Felon may soon go by the moniker, Fiancé Frank. The arsonist turned out to be a man from out of the area, who loved fires, and seized on the opportunity of a vacant and controversial condo project. Not only was he not connected with any radical environmental groups, he'd received two citations in the past for littering.

It's probably too soon to say whether Marti and Frank will be happily ever aftering it, but it looks like there's a good chance of it.

My good friend Henry Greeley, went out on his boating date, sporting his new leather jacket. He enjoyed himself but is still searching for his soul mate.

As for me, a large parade was organized and I sat atop a throne in my mended and dry cleaned ruffled pink flower girl's dress, waving and throwing kisses to the masses. They'd come together to celebrate their good fortune that appraisers reside among them and to watch as I was presented a key to the city from Detective Camille Costas.

On a more real note, Mrs. Stirnaman is back home. It's wonderful to have her back as a neighbor but I had to relinquish Julian. I still have visitation rights and we often go for long walks together. Meanwhile, I've been researching dog breeds and dog rescue websites. I can't wait to find my own canine companion. As for Ben Parks, Mrs. Stirnaman's doctor, he did call me, almost certainly as a result of her urging. We met up for a run and coffee one morning. He is a great guy and hopefully that was the start of a good friendship.

But the best part, is that a fork lift came zipping down my street today with ribbons tied around the front struts. At the controls was Rick Sommers, cradling an armful of red and yellow Gerbera daisies.

Recipes

For your cooking and dining pleasure, I have included a few original recipes. I hope you like them.

This is my dad's original recipe. It's fun to make and good to eat but just don't spill the sauce on your leg.

Duke's Pizza

Crust

1/2 teaspoon yeast

3/4 cup warm water (yeast temperature)

4 teaspoons sugar

2 cups flour

4 teaspoons vegetable oil

3 tablespoons dried milk

Put the yeast and sugar into the warm water and set aside. In a medium size mixing bowl, combine the flour, vegetable oil, dried milk and salt. Mix. When you notice that the yeast has become active, pour it into the flour mixture. Stir and add a bit more water or flour if it is needed. If possible, refrigerate for one to four hours. The dough will rise a bit and be easier to work with. When ready, place the dough in a greased pizza pan and stretch it to fit the pan. A rolling pin can help.

Pizza sauce

1/4 cup tomato paste

1-2 teaspoons oregano

Dash of sugar

1/4 teaspoon garlic powder

1/4 teaspoon pepper

Combine all of the above in a small mixing bowl then spread on the pizza crust. Top with cheeses and toppings. I usually use a combination of shredded mozzarella, shredded sharp cheddar and feta.

Bake at 450 degrees for about 12-15 minutes or until the bottom of the crust is browned slightly.

This recipe is from my good friend, Nick. If you try them and like them, great. If you don't then pay no more heed to meat recipes given to you by a vegetarian.

Nick's Burgers

2 pounds ground sirloin

1/4 pound ground sausage

One package instant onion soup mix

Salt and pepper to taste

Mix everything together and shape into patties of a desired size. I wear disposable plastic gloves for this part of the procedure but you may okay with slathering beef all over your hands. Grill or fry to desired state of doneness.

Optional Blue Cheese Burger

Shape two thinner patties and make an indentation in one. Place the desired amount of blue cheese in the hollowed out area. Place the second patty on top and crimp the edges together.

World's Best Peanut Butter Cookies

- 1 Cup brown sugar, firmly packed
- 1 Cup white sugar
- 1 Cup butter
- 1 and 1/4 cup peanut butter*
- 1 teaspoon vanilla
- 2 eggs, beaten
- 3 Cups flour
- 2 teaspoons baking soda
- 1 teaspoon salt

*It really does matter whether you use good quality peanut butter. It's best to use a kind that only consists of salt and peanuts.

Combine all of the ingredients and stir until well mixed. Shape into balls about one inch in diameter. Flatten in a cross pattern with a table fork. Bake at 325 degrees for about 12 to 15 minutes. Don't over bake. One recipe makes about 70 cookies. It is wise to triple the recipe.

Stake Out Take Out

1/4 Cup canola oil

1 Teaspoon mustard seeds

1 and 1/2 Teaspoons cumin

1/2 Teaspoon seasoning salt

1 Teaspoon sugar

3/4 Teaspoon chili powder (not cayenne)

1 Teaspoon garam masala

1/4 Teaspoon cayenne pepper

1 Teaspoon Worcestershire sauce

1 Cup dry roasted salted peanuts

1 Cup Rice Krispies

1 Cup corn flakes

3 Cups Chex cereal

Heat the mustard seeds in a large pan until the seeds pop, about two minutes. Turn off the heat. Add cumin, salt, sugar, chili powder, garam masala, cayenne pepper and Worcestershire sauce (there is a vegetarian version if you want to avoid those annoying anchovies) and stir for about one minute. Add the peanuts and again stir for a minute. Add all of the cereals and mix well. Season to taste. Serves about twelve people at a party or one on a stake-out.

Connie Doherty lives in northwestern Lower Michigan where on some days the air is so fresh it has never been breathed. When she's not writing or appraising, she loves to walk with her dog, kayak, paddle board, roller blade, cross country ski, cook, and eat.

Hot Property is the first book in a "hot" new series. Coming soon: Hot Dog.